THE DEMANDS

Drew Geraci

Dedicated to Barbara Leech

It's your life
And you can do what you want

1

Thwaang.

"Aaaaahh . . . Shit," Laney muttered.

The last B-string on her used Yamaha guitar, broken.

She really wanted to rail at the top of her lungs, but it was close to midnight. Her tenant agreement included no loud noises, especially after dark. No sense in waking up Margo, her elderly neighbor in the adjacent loft above the bar, Blackie's. She practiced with her amp at a very low volume.

It was also best not to let outsiders know she was home. The neighborhood was lousy with prostitutes and drug dealers. Having no windows kept the curious away.

She rummaged around the boxes of spare strings to no avail, fuming with impatience and pent up frustration. The boxes of strings he bought for her. It was Sunday night, so there was no music equipment store open. Just when she was about to nail The Kinks' "Tired of Waiting for You," straight through without messing up.

The irony of the song title was not lost on her. Todd was tired of waiting too. For her. Sure, she still had some residual affection for him, but he was tired of humoring her, always taking second place to her rock star ambitions. Todd's ambitions never extended beyond partying all weekend, his reward for what he considered a hard work week. Paying for that box of strings was his entire investment in her career path. His emotional investment, even less.

"Hmm," she hmm'ed to herself.

It was time to call it a night anyway. She'd have to resume tomorrow. The print shop wasn't going to open itself. She never showed up late to work, much to the derision of certain coworkers. The same coworkers who always needed her to spot them until payday. The same coworkers who whined when she asked for her money back. Both the owner and the manager probably started Signs That Sell with the romanticism of self-employment, but somewhere along the way, they never factored in hard work. That meant the shop could lose customers or close permanently. That meant no work and no job for Laney. Since moving to Pittsburgh from Maryland on her own, Laney had developed A-type mental muscles. The burden of running the shop fell squarely on her shoulders.

Monday morning, the alarm phone app jabbed her out of her REM sleep. Alone. Turn the coffee pot on, a quick shower, dress, shove some toast in her mouth, fill the travel mug, race down the steps, beat the traffic.

There were two customers waiting outside Signs That Sell when she unlocked the door and turned on the lights.

It was a rough day, even for a Monday. She finished a long-standing order on time. Rush orders included vinyl lettering for business vehicles and grand opening banners. She skipped lunch again. Kelly forgot to reorder grommets. This, among other things, kept Laney a whirling dervish until closing. The fellow employees were only in the way. The silver lining was that the eight hours seemed to fly by.

Her more agreeable coworkers made plans to see Monday Night Football at a sports bar. The Ravens versus the Browns. Tempting, but no. Her lack of funds helped in the decision-making process. But she did have enough to buy B-strings after closing Signs That Sell. She was back in business. The business she wanted to belong to one day.

Still wired from the busy day, her anticipation for guitar playing was now irresistible. No time for naysayers while off-the-clock. Dan, the coworker who mocked her daily for being a girl "play-acting as a rock star" didn't even get to her today. Over the months, she had developed a coping mechanism to deal with Dan while playing at home. She warmed up every practice with a song she'd secretly written about him.

> *I know a guy named Dickhead Dan*
> *Dickhead Dan*
> *Dickhead Dan*

She tried to come up with more lyrics, but just singing that ditty was enough. Why waste more mental shelf space on that loser? It became more of a mantra to help relax and get her vocal chords to loosen while she tuned up. She usually smiled during that song. Straight-up garage guitar-oriented rock music was the only thing that made her feel alive. It was her energy drink. While her childhood friends gushed over boy bands, she had a crush on Jack White and his dark, discordant songs. The shearing noise from his guitar was both disturbing and hypnotic. Plus, his drummer was a girl. Making a living doing what they did was a long shot in an era of Country, Hip-Hop and committee-style pop recordings for marginal talents much prettier than she. She had no kick against modern jazz, that is, unless they played it too darn fast.

She was petite with cute, pixie-like features, in a manner that guys described as "attainable," as if it were a compliment.

Her hair, dubbed dirty blonde, hung to the small of her back, kept in a ponytail more often than not. Her fingernails were short and stubby, due to years of strumming with her fingers rather than using a pick. She had a strong sense of self for someone so young. Tonight the only time thoughts of Todd entered her mind was when she threw the empty guitar string box in the trash. His last gift to her. She'd have to do a lot more cleaning to dispense of all things Todd in her tiny apartment. But not tonight. Thank God she'd never taken his offer to move in with him. His was a nicer neighborhood with all the trappings, but from his demeanor, she felt he would consider her another piece of furniture. Settling down sounded great, but not now. And certainly not with Todd. His dismissal of her talent made the breakup somewhat easier. If she didn't have feelings for him, she'd have broken up sooner. But he was a hindrance and she knew it was the right thing to do.

Three evening practice sessions and a payday later, she permitted herself to toss back a beer or two during another open mike night at The Hotseat. Once she entered through the back entrance of the building, dodging urine stains and new faces selling the same drugs, she would see a variety of debuting acts. Some nights, comedians, other nights, musicians. The Hotseat was an underground club, populated with amped-up hecklers like those of the legendary Apollo Theater, only more vicious. Here, artists had little time to win the crowd over. Word around town was that if you received the slightest sign of approval at The Hotseat, you had what it took to make it big. The word was specifically aimed at incautious amateurs. Setting up tenpins.

Laney entered halfway through a song being played by a Glam Shock Rock act. The pale, rawboned, glitter-wearing leader and his band borrowed heavily from The Dolls, Alice Cooper and Marilyn Manson. He was in-your-face in a way that he knew would piss off the crowd. Sure enough, catcalls cued his removal. He was dragged away kicking and screaming, but oversold it and came off as phony. Laney may not have cared for his music or act, but she respected his sheer audacity.

Another, younger man was shoved out from the backstage and he played James Taylor songs to the best of his ability, to a lukewarm reception. His singing was sincere, but his guitar playing was nowhere near as accomplished as Taylor's. The audience, apparently mollified by music they were familiar with, enjoyed the folksinger's self-deprecating humor between songs as well. A serviceable performance, which only garnered a few heckles. Laney soaked it all in like a beer-soaked rag. She knew deep down she had untapped potential, but how to convince a crowd of bored, hostile and drunk strangers to accept what she had to offer?

2

Mitch Slater flopped the last magazine to the floor of his hospital room. His parents meant well, but issues of *Sports Focus* and *Celebrity Insider* were far from his field of interests. He tried hard to scan for something, *anything*, that interested him, but they were all the same periodicals he ignored when he'd get his tires rotated. He was past caring if the sound of the magazine landing woke up the patient next to him, Jack, who was recovering from a quadruple bypass, amongst other ailments. Mitch had lost his MP3 player and daytime TV offerings of smug talk show hosts lecturing ignoramuses about common sense solutions just made Mitch more depressed.

Mitch's pallor had gotten worse, from too much time spent indoors. He usually had light olive skin that really made for a good tan in summer. His black, wispy hair had grown long and he began growing a beard. His features were unremarkable, save for the strong jawline he'd gotten from his grandfather on his mother's side.

At least his severe pneumonia had cleared and he was being weaned off the meds he'd taken for the past month. Mitch's boredom finally drove him to cautiously hoist himself off the bed so he could walk around in the hopes of lessening his feeling of sensory deprivation. Despite the physical therapy, his walking was still wobbly so he braced against the walls to stay upright. His body had atrophied somewhat during his stay. He was only 29, but he felt twice his age. He'd gamble that the people at the nurses' station were capable of conversation beyond whatever new accomplishments their kids achieved. When that inevitable topic would arise, Mitch would manipulate the discussion to something he could relate to.

Mitch's case of pneumonia had gone from life-threatening to stable. He would soon leave this sterile, docile environment and resume a normal life. Aside from the occasional visitor providing him company, Mitch's pastime was reevaluating his life.

He would have died, but for the quick treatment Dr. Shim had administered. Fortunately, Dr. Shim, one of the state's best, was also the doctor for the Pittsburgh Steelers. Although Mitch's condition had been successfully treated, it was only a symptom of some greater malady, which remained elusive. Mitch had no recollection of any event that placed him in the hospital. The best that could be done at this point was for Mitch to follow through with his post-recovery appointments and for Shim to share his case files with specialists more qualified to diagnose Mitch's mystery ailment.

Mitch's advertising job seemed so trivial now. The 14-hour days he relentlessly toiled, just to keep the treadmill running, were not good. Oddly enough, his hospital roommate had also been in advertising for decades. Seeing the toll the years had taken on him was a window into Mitch's future. Something had to change. If only he could nail down what he would do upon reentering society.

Finally, Mitch's dad, Richard, found the MP3 player. It had fallen between some boxes containing Mitch's belongings in the guest room. When Mitch's parents had seen him at death's door, they'd made arrangements. They excavated the contents of his apartment and placed it in their garage. Richard stumbled upon the MP3 player while looking for the long-overdue library book that Mitch mentioned needed returning, of all things. Sometimes solving small problems helped Richard block out the larger problems. He became a hero when he reunited Mitch with his MP3 player. Richard then began telling Mitch about his discovery of the MP3 player at great length, often going off on tangents that seemingly trailed off forever. Mitch's mind raced, mentally wishing his dad would wrap up his stories and leave, so Mitch could listen to his music. But Richard had raised his son to be patient, thus Mitch listened with feigned engagement, hearing key words then responding with short comments, with hopes that Dad would get the hint. Dad had brought the MP3 player, after all, so Mitch white-knuckled one dull story after another. What seemed like hours passed before Mitch was again alone. Mitch's demeanor improved greatly when he turned on his MP3 player. Its purpose was twofold: Drowning out the hospital's loudspeakers interspersed with hallway chatter and moans; and losing himself in his favorite songs.

3

Laney was making another pilgrimage to The Hotseat. Why was she drawn to a dank vortex of broken dreams, where insulting someone's first outing was a sport? She had Todd to thank for taking her here the first time, strictly as a lark. Todd knew the owner, so she was still allowed access alone. That first visit was the stuff of nightmares. Todd showed his gentlemanly side at first, introducing her to the regulars. Once the show started, she soon learned the true purpose of The Hotseat: A mean-spirited version of the *Gong Show*. Instead of the talent engaging members of the audience, the talent was subject to ridicule that built to a fevered pitch, forcing the talent off the stage, sometimes in tears. Laney at first thought it was amusing, if disturbing. Todd, on the other hand, clapped and shrieked like a gibbon. There was the juggling comedian who heavily borrowed one-liners that even the worst hack comedians wouldn't have touched—he lasted almost two minutes. The next act was a pale, middle-aged, freckled woman with a pink streak in her otherwise blonde hair. She wore a peasant blouse with a denim skirt and brown leather boots, stepping onto the stage, holding a violin and bow in a death grip. She quietly cleared her throat, then an audience member, eager to start the festivities, shouted: "Take off your top!" The violinist appeared unfazed and began flawlessly playing Max Bruch's violin concerto number 3 in D minor, a difficult and rare treat on any stage. The Hotseat crowd didn't know from culture and let the insults fly. The violinist kept playing through the din of thoughtless taunts and tossed beer coasters. She began jabbing louder on the violin and the tempo of her playing sped up, knowing her time would be short. Even the women, who Laney assumed would take pity, drunkenly chimed insults amongst the calamity. Laney had long ago stopped smiling. *This was not a lark, this was a lynching.*

On the walk home, Todd, several beers in him, felt the afterglow of what he considered an entertaining night. Beside him, Laney tucked her hands in her pockets, quietly brooding. When Todd finally noticed, he repeatedly asked her what was wrong. After she responded, "Nothing," four times, the questions stopped. There were times he could be really sweet, and other times glaringly insensitive. This was the worst side she'd seen of him yet. As pissed as she was at Todd, she was more disgusted with herself, sitting on the sidelines while boors verbally trampled a gifted musician off the stage. She was probably someone's mother, looking for a way to break from her everyday existence, learning an elaborate piece of classical music to express herself. Someone's idea of a joke was to steer her to the wrong venue.

4

Laney's goals as a rock star were outrageously lofty, but every success starts with a germ of an idea, she assured herself. There were gamers who simulated playing classic rock songs on faux guitars, so there had to be a market to tap into, right? Depending on the day, her mood could weave between excitement and sullenness. It was crazy ambitious, but if not now, when?

During her teens, Laney preferred staying home with her guitar while her few friends enjoyed the constant pulse of nightclub techno music. Her bedroom was surrounded by posters of many classic rock legends, most of them dead before her time, dead before their time. She'd always been the misfit, who liked "weird music," according to others her age. She'd tried sharing obscure songs from known acts, but the response was a bored "I only like the hits." Apparently, a lot of people liked chewing on the same musical cud as comfort food.

Since she was a child, something about power chords triggered something in her that nothing else could. She couldn't get enough of books that covered the history of rock music, from the roots of Robert Johnson, Elvis, Chuck Berry, R&B, the British Invasion, punk rock, grunge and beyond. She couldn't get enough of it and it made her sad to think she was born too late. Her passion lay in a bygone era, when rock music was the shit, filling arenas, even stadiums. But Laney had the conceit of youth to believe she'd give the breath of life to rock 'n' roll, making it mainstream again. Any other interests were a distant second.

At twenty-two, Laney moved away from her family's Laurel, Maryland home to somewhere, anywhere else, that she might find this longshot dream. Three years prior, Dad passed away in his sleep, only forty-nine years old, an ignoble way to go for a decorated soldier. Laney's older brother, Terry, remained in their house. Mom's special crab cakes kept him content and he assumed the traditional man of the house role, fixing light switches, hefting heavy objects and such. Laney had grown restless and felt stagnated in this comfy womb. Her neighborhood friends were off to college, and the few times she visited them, she was more the outsider than before. She was tired of fielding questions about what major she was taking and which college she attended.

She learned of other high school graduates who jumped into college right away, only to eventually crash and burn, valuing parties to studies. At her lowest ebb, Laney had designs for some manner of trade school, but gave herself time post-graduation to think things through. She fought to ignore Catherine and Terry's prodding to either start school or search for a proper job.

Baltimore had a good music scene, but it became stale to her. Familiarity breeds contempt and all that. There was really no reason to stay. Her favorite writers accrued material from a gypsy lifestyle, so it made sense to her. Piddling around in her room was getting her nowhere and she needed new experiences.

5

When the day arrived, Catherine Barbara Kilburn couldn't hold back the tears while waving goodbye as her daughter's ratty Toyota, overloaded with belongings, left the driveway. Whittling down said belongings for the exodus had been far more difficult than Laney expected, leaving only her guitar, amp, clothes, blanket, pillow and some necessities for the kitchen and bathroom.

She didn't have a particular destination in mind, but chose I-270 North to I-70 west where the open highway would give her time to ponder. Hours into her road trip to nowhere, she came down from the high of her brazen move and fought temptation to turn back home.

Many potholes later, she saw signs beckoning travelers to visit Pittsburgh, Pennsylvania. During one pee break, she chanced upon a flea market next to a gas station. She found some good swag: scuffed cassettes she could play in the car. Robert Cray. Nick Cave and The Bad Seeds. The Pretenders, to replace the last three copies she'd worn out. She always followed its instructions PLAY THIS ALBUM LOUD, much to the consternation of her parents. Chrissie Hynde was her role model. The first time she saw a girl fronting an all male band. Not only that, they kicked major ass. Her doubts began to wilt, the new cassettes starting the soundtrack for her new life. The idea of making it on her own, not giving a shit, was freeing.

She couldn't resist when the Pittsburgh exit drew near.

Laney asked the toll booth worker about areas of Pittsburgh she could afford on the cheap. She learned that Pittsburgh was not necessarily specific to just the city limits, but denoted many small townships proudly considering themselves extensions of Pittsburgh. She found this village neighborhood unique as she drove about.

So many small mill towns. Some warm and cozy-looking with well-trimmed lawns the size of a couch. She had also passed mill towns long-abandoned since steel became outsourced. She envisioned a steel-wool tumbleweed crossing her path. She'd read online there was a burgeoning bohemian music scene in Pittsburgh and wanted to check it out. This feeling of unfamiliarity filled her with electricity. Most importantly, Pittsburgh was far more affordable than the Beltway region she'd left. New York City would have to wait a while. Laney rationalized, if this would be the place she'd plant herself, it was only a four-hour drive from her mother.

After a very long day of driving and gulping down fast food, Laney called it a night when she spotted a motel that looked like something she could afford with some modicum of safety, with its well-lit outdoor parking area. Mom made do with her mid-level administrative job, but paying for an apartment for Laney was not in her budget. Also, she made it clear to Laney that once she left on her own, there was no moving back. Mom meant exactly what she said . . . at that moment. Chances were, she'd renege, just to have her baby back home and safe.

6

Waking in an unfamiliar bed in a strange town was discon-
certing. Laney sprang up and began gasping. She was having
an anxiety attack. What was she thinking, going out on her
own in a place where she knew nobody? Fighting the instinct
to pull the bed covers over her head, she flailed her small
frame from the bed, jammed her boots on, and then took a
few strides out the hallway to the elevator. This dump promoted its free continental breakfast and by God, she was going to
load herself up before she went out again. If someone thought
she was a crazy person in her jammies, Doc Martens and a
bad case of bedhead, all the better. She wasn't in the mood for
conversation. The runny eggs, stale Danishes and burnt coffee
began to help her feel centered. With each gulp, she felt her
blood sugar coming back.

After checking out, Laney resumed her travels, feeling a
bit queasy. Maybe she should have skipped the extra Danish.
This day was a substantial contrast to the twenty-four hours
prior. Unfamiliar settings and a tummy ache. Laney listened to
the local radio stations. There was a need to absorb as much
information about Pittsburgh if this was to be her potential
new home.

Her day was consumed by driving around, looking for
apartments. All of them either too pricey (but not Maryland
pricey) or in areas where the term "dump" would be generous.
The day ended a total wash-out. Another cheap motel for the

night chipped away at her savings. This continental breakfast was an improvement from the previous motel. The lack of both plastic forks and knowledge from staff as to finding more was the least of her concerns. A plastic spoon and knife would have to do.

Day three she pressed on. The area was an M.C. Escher rendering brought to life. Roads wove through untamed hills with water rolling over the rocks. Many a steep slope would spring just around a corner. A far cry from the flat streets she grew up on. She'd looked over guardrails to learn she'd somehow found herself hundreds of feet above a spot she'd driven twenty minutes ago. She was seeing a side of Pittsburgh she hadn't expected. Her preconception of the area being purely industrial was wrong. Thickets of trees gave her an odd sense of welcome. The mix of urban and agricultural spots filled her head with possibilities.

"Driving around here must be a bitch in the winter," she said to her indifferent Toyota. She crossed the Highland Park Bridge over the Allegheny River. At the end of the bridge were tentacles of exits, and by now, she was road-weary. She randomly chose the Sharpsburg exit. She was running out of patience, and more importantly, gasoline. It was only midday, but the thought of getting stuck in yet another commuter jam would send her into an emotional tailspin. She had saved some money for this trip, but it was finite and indulging in more travel seemed wasteful at this point.

Sharpsburg was a very small town, comprised of less than one square mile. At the intersection of Main and Canal Street stood the tall, proud statue of Guyasuta, leader of the Seneca people. She took it as a sign that Guyasuta petitioned her to stay. Sharpsburg appeared to have an easy access point to other towns, considering the bus line. That would come in handy if finances really got tight. Sharpsburg had probably thrived with mom & pop stores once, but it now had just enough businesses to function. The classic architecture of the places of worship, crammed into this small town, impressed her greatly. In her adult life, Laney only attended church during funerals and weddings, but there was no denying the glory of the majestic craftsmanship. Of all the other towns she'd passed, this one struck a chord with her. She didn't question it. Gotta start somewhere.

She'd gone this far without relying on a map or the GPS app on her phone. Her credit cards had nearly maxed out, the aftermath of foolish teenage years. For the most part, she was off the grid. She emptied her Maryland bank account and brought what little savings she had, carefully stashed away.

7

Laney found one apartment's placement oddly appealing and surely affordable: above a small, ramshackle bar. This bar had no name, it seemed. Unless it was called Apartment for Rent. The rent sign, faded from the sun, was still legible. Sure it was a bar, but it looked more like a clubhouse for retirees, a less rowdy clientele, based on the many bumper stickers proclaiming various war veteran statuses. Probably just enough regulars to keep the Open sign lit. Pittsburgh supposedly had the most bars per capita in the country. All the ones she passed hadn't necessarily disproved that, so what was one more? Maybe she could eventually showcase here then crash to her room above afterwards. Many optimistic thoughts, even stupid ones, had raced through her head the past few days, prompted by this surge of adventure.

The Toyota's transmission groaned as she parked. She undid the ponytail that had made her look much younger than she was. Before she could enter the bar, out lumbered a heavy-set, yet muscular 60-ish man with leathery, craggy features that made Laney's thoughts immediately spring to images of pirates. He had deep crow's feet that looked like the result of fish hooks boring into his temples. He wore a pink polo shirt and faded blue jeans. What little grey hair he had was combed over in an attempt to stay a few years younger. He and Laney grew slightly closer in age through their respective grooming efforts.

•   •   •

"So what brings a pretty young thing like you here? If it's a summons, Blackie takes care of that sort of thing. I'm just his eyes, ears, and sometimes, muscle."

Laney, standing as straight, tall and assured as she could, said: "Um, is that apartment still for rent?"

"Yinz from HUD? We're up to code, thanks to a grand worth of upgrades n'at." He scratched his armpit as he looked her up and down.

"So you're saying that the apartment is available?"

"'At's what I'm sayin'."

"How much?"

"Fer *you*? I don't think this's your kinda scene, kid."

"Can I at least look at the apartment and decide for myself?"

He walked towards the side of the building, motioning with a hand for her to follow.

"Sure, but don't expect Barbie's Dream House."

Such expectations never entered her mind. But upgrades sounded promising. There was a black metal staircase that led to the second story. His footsteps on the staircase were a thunderous sound, making small talk pointless.

At the top of the stairs there was a recently-painted olive green door. Who still uses olive green, she thought with a shrug. Laney let the big man enter the darkened room first, in case she needed to run back down the stairs screaming.

"There she is! Got the plumbing working, new stove, actually a refurbished stove, but it works fine."

The big man pulled a chain in the middle of what passed for the dining area. A bare bulb lit up. She could now scan the room. And what a room it was. An attic apartment with unfinished hardwood flooring and a hasty paint job throughout.

At least it was white, not olive green. Most of the utilities were old, but good old. At least fifty years old, when things were built to last. An old radiator, that some would consider a kitsch collectable, stood in the center of the unfurnished living room. The tap water ran clear, not brown, a good sign. Aside from the dining area and bathroom, there was only room for a kitchenette and a bed in the opposite corner. 300 square feet of apartment. This was a long drop from her parent's comfy ranch house, but it *did* look very affordable. Ages ago, this may have been storage space until the previous bar owner added the amenities to keep his home and business in one place.

"The rent's three hunnert bucks on the fifteenth of each month. Utilities are covered."

Laney choked back a stammer, assessing rapidly if this was a deal or too much for such small living quarters in Pittsburgh.

"Aside from the shitter, excuse me, bathroom, you see the whole place in this one room. No attic or crawlspaces to store stuff. You'll need your own furniture. I got some wood in the back if you want shelves. Previous tenant took his bookshelf with 'im."

"Why'd he leave?"

"Girlfriend got knocked up, so he moved t' North Hills t' be with her. Don't know if they got married or not. I ain't the nebby type. So many babies havin' babies these days with no ring. World's a mess anymore."

The big man's grousing caused Laney to become dour. Maybe this was a mistake. But maybe . . .

"Two hundred and fifty dollars."

"No."

"Two seventy-five."

"No. You're gettin' a break as I'm not asking for a deposit."

Suddenly Laney was playing *The Price Is Right*.

"I don't know if I can go higher than that. I'm strapped for cash but I'm going to look for a job tomorrow."

"No job? Forget it."

"Wait!"

"I said forget it."

"What if I pay you earnest money up front? Two hundred dollars plus fifty dollars deposit right now?"

She just told a stranger she had at least $250 on her person. She stopped breathing for a long time before she realized it and released the air from her lungs as quietly as possible.

Dumb dumb dumb, she thought. The big man scratched his armpit again.

"Cash?"

Laney threw caution and a good bit of her sanity to the wind.

"Cash."

"Tell ya what, I've always been good at readin' people, and you seem so sweet and innocent . . . I figured you for a suburban girl and could get three hunnert from you. Two hunnert's good. Never mind the deposit. Somethin' tells me you'll need it."

He stood still as she approached him. Then she placed two hundred dollars in his heavily callused hand.

Once the money touched his hand, he snatched it away in the blink of an eye, then crouched in a threatening stance.

"Uuuh! Uh!" were the only sounds her vocal chords could squeak out.

The big man stood upright, resumed his casual stance and pointed at her.

"Gotcha, kid! You ain't a screamer and you almost looked like you could almost stand your ground. You gotta work on that!"

Laney retained a standing position, but teetered a bit.

"Name's Vic."

"Dih-uuh. Huh!" Her heart beat faster than she'd known possible. She huffed as she fought another anxiety attack. She hadn't been prone to anxiety attacks until she moved away. This one was at least justified. Working very hard at calming oneself down is both a chore and a contradiction. Ride the wave. To calm herself down, she closed her eyes, surrendering to whatever fate had in store for her that moment. When she opened her eyes, she saw Vic still in the same pose. She'd passed some sort of test. She began to feel like herself again. But a new, bolder version of herself. This experience had to eventually take the form of one of her songs, making lemons into lemon zest, or whatever.

"Eleanor. But I hate it so I go by Laney."

"Nice to meet you, Laney. I didn't think yinz had it in you to dicker over the rent, but well played, kid. One last thing, there's another apartment attached to the other side. She's an old widow named Margo. She never leaves. Blackie checks in with her ev'ry day. Her family almost never visits. Blackie's more family than her own flesh-and-blood. So no loud parties."

After handing Laney the key, Vic turned, exiting the door.

Laney watched Vic plod down the stairs. At the bottom, Vic turned back and bellowed as he pointed at her.

"But remember! Two hunnert by the fifteenth of each month, or I'll toss ya out on your ass!" Through his pronouncement, Vic grew a wide smile. He headed to the front of the bar.

Laney entered her new apartment and locked the door handle, then the puny chain lock. The early punk rock regulars she admired from New York's CBGB club had started out with humble beginnings, too. Sleeping in single-room apartments, sharing mattresses, so this was a step above, she consoled herself. But CBGBs was no more. She shook off such negative thoughts and she snapped into a newfound default setting: problem-solving. First, find a job, second, a mattress and stronger locks. Tonight she had a roof over her head full of songs.

8

Back at his parent's home in West Mifflin, Mitch devoured pasta e fagioli and bracioli like a man being sent to the electric chair. A man blocking out the memory of hospital food. His mother knew it was his favorite and prepared it as a home-coming meal. Mitch had grown up in a mixed family. Despite the Britannic surname, his mother, formerly Rose Ciolli, was the full-blooded Italian matriarch of the family. When Richard Slater proposed to her thirty-odd years ago, Rose thought she'd never hear the end of the teasing, marrying someone so . . . non-Italian. Richard appreciated Rose's fiery spirit when it came to both strong opinions and compassion. Rose respected Richard's calm reassurances in trying times. Yin and yang.

Hours later, Mitch was still feeling bloated from the splendid meal. He then dropped the bomb on his parents that he wanted to change careers and start over, which was met with explosive criticism.

"Ma, I'll be fine!"

Rose wagged a finger for emphasis.

"What you put your father and I through! I—"

Her head down, she swallowed her next words. She raised a closed fist which unfolded into an open-palmed stop sign.

For twenty seconds, time and space stood still.

"You cannot do this to us. You finally got a good paying job and you want to throw it away? For what?"

"All that time in the hospital—"

"That cost us a fortune! Not that, thank the Blessed Mother, we're not happy you're better, but—"

"Look, I had a lot of downtime and being sick for so long got me thinking. Is this what it's all about? Slaving away at a job that I hate?"

"A good paying job! A lot of people would kill for a job in advertising, sitting around with fun ideas and getting paid for it!"

"Ma, I don't get paid for ideas. I get paid for pushing papers, making budgets, chasing merchandisers for last-minute prices before publication! Nobody respects me 'cause I'm the youngest exec there!"

"So you should take pride in your job that much more!"

"I do! I do! It's just . . ."

Rose folded her arms, staring away, trying to contain herself.

"Am I gonna end up like my hospital roommate, wired up and tested every half hour? Christ, I can't even remember his name!"

Rose took the opportunity of hearing the Lord's name to make the sign of the cross. Mitch bristled at his mother's obvious attempts to silence him by pouring on the Catholic guilt. She wasn't usually this over-the-top. Richard, as was his usual reaction, stayed on the sidelines, letting Rose do the talking for both of them.

"That'll be me one day, someone you spend months sharing a hospital room with whose miserable job robbed him of his spirit. His kids barely visited him, and you can tell they did so out of obligation."

"That will never be you, Mitchell! You have a lot of family who love and take pride in you!" Rose popped back.

Mitch buried his face in his fists.

"God, I hate my job. Things were easier when I first started there, but they kept promoting me, and the money kept me wantin' to climb that stupid corporate ladder."

"That's the medication they gave you talking!"

9

The following week, Mitch was given a clean bill of health to return to work, so he did. His dress shirt hung looser due to the weight loss during his hospital stay. The office was in an isolated industrial park, consisting of beige and grey buildings, the only bright colors originating from corporate logos.

Eschewing the elevator as he always did, Mitch trudged up three flights of stairs (which he justified as part of his daily cardio) to enter his office. When he started working at Devinshire Concepts, he used to strut up those same stairs, two at a time. He couldn't recall exactly when this routine became a slow Bataan Death March. He'd leave late every night, another little chunk of his soul chipped away. Maybe the time away would be a fresh start. Each person he passed welcomed him back with handshakes and hugs, not all of them sincere.

When Mitch approached his small, but private office he met his nemesis, Chris Horton.

Chris leapt up from Mitch's chair with his predictable phoniness.

"Hey, big guy! Look at you! Looks like you're back in the game!"

Chris' first language was football-coach-speak. He offered Mitch a fist bump which was reciprocated out of habit more than enthusiasm.

"Hey . . . Chris. Didn't know they chose you. Must be movin' on up."

"It's been hell covering your division, but I think you'll like the improvements I added to help you out, champ! But before we get to that, Leon wants to see you."

Mitch only met with Leon when there was a problem. Perhaps Leon subverted his natural state for a perfunctory welcome back.

Leon Bates was a jowly, red-nosed, suspender-wearing brute whose epidermis housed only meanness and gravy.

"Hi, Leon."

"Have a seat!"

Mitch plopped down on one of the two leather chairs in front of Leon's obscenely-large oak desk.

Leon leaned back in his chair, his hands folded behind his head. Mitch couldn't help but notice that in this pose, Leon's bellybutton was showing between his shirt buttons.

"First of all, glad you're back on your feet. But that's not why I called you here."

Uh oh, Mitch thought.

"Chris tells me that your office, accounts and computer files were a fucking mess and he worked day and night just to get some sort of order. He's suggested ways to run your division more efficiently and I can't disagree with him."

Mitch struggled not to stare at that bellybutton. This oaf was holding court with his bellybutton sticking out.

"Now I'm going easy on you because you just got back, but I expect this transition to be easier than the mess you left Chris. Do we understand each other, Slater?"

All lies.

Mitch was fastidious about keeping his records protected, yet accessible to others who would cover his accounts when he took time off. His protocols were so well documented, even an intern could cover for him. During his hospital stay, there was little room for error, except human error. And Chris was the definition of human error. Chris was always the first to show up for work, and the last to leave, as he proudly pointed out on a daily basis. Not that he got much done in his long days. It was purely for show. After all, there were funny pet videos that needed his attention. Everyone knew it except Leon, who served more as a figurehead than an actual boss. Leon was out of touch about who did what. All he knew about Chris was the long hours and that was enough to impress him.

Kangaroo court was in session. Mitch girded himself, preparing to verbally question the veracity of his character witness and request all charges be dismissed. He had successfully stood his ground in the past, the result always a stalemate. All that wasted energy, just for the honor of continued employment at Devinshire Concepts. His talents were either overlooked, undermined, or exploited by coworkers like Chris who'd lay claim to Mitch's best accomplishments. When the futility sank in, Mitch's plans for rebuttal were wiped clean as a shaken Etch A Sketch.

Mitch's fixation elevated from Leon's exposed bellybutton to his eyes. Mitch sat up casually before resting his elbows on Leon's desk, resting his chin on his clasped hands, never losing eye contact. This unexpected move disarmed Leon.

"Leon . . ."

"Ever had a priest say your last rites? I have."

Mitch continued unblinkingly staring Leon down. The redness of Leon's nose spread to the rest of his face. Leon was used to being the most alpha of males and unfamiliar with insubordination.

"You need me more than I need you."

"Now I could do you a huge favor by giving two weeks' notice, or I can leave now. Your call."

"Now!" Leon howled as he abruptly stood up. The howl was more out of embarrassment than rage. Mitch spoiled Leon's plans for a good dressing down. Mitch rose and casually opened the office door. Before leaving, Mitch turned back to Leon.

"And for Christ's sake, wear an undershirt. It's hard to be authoritative with your bellybutton on display." Once Mitch closed the door, Leon knocked items off his desk. Items that included small framed photographs of him, smiling with his family.

Mitch didn't bother to stop at his office to collect the few personal items that adorned his workspace. He hadn't missed them while he was gone a month and he could always get a new Star Wars coffee mug.

Upon reaching the exit, he met Dwayne Simons, one of the few coworkers Mitch confided in.

"You come back just to leave?"

"I'll tell you sometime, over a beer. Just watch your back. You excel here, you're a target."

Dwayne watched him leave, perplexed by Mitch's cryptic words.

10

Many a person leaves the French Riviera with a healthy tan, feeling rested and rewarded. Not so for Arthur Peters, whose birth name was Artur Petrov. Broad-shouldered, paunchy with unnaturally dark hair for a man his age. He enjoyed his vacations but hated coming back to Pittsburgh to face another harsh winter. He was a good earner and never complained to the higher-ups. Too good an earner. His bosses needed him to stay in Pittsburgh. Why mess with success? Arthur's displeasure had mounted the past few years. He'd seen younger men promoted before him and his resentment grew. These punks hadn't put in the time Arthur did. It was unfair. On his flight home, Arthur wracked his brain over improving his situation. He had been told his Pittsburgh time would be temporary. That was a decade ago and now he felt he was merely a placeholder. Something had to change.

11

Laney woke up painfully, her left shoulder stiff from sleeping on the floor. She'd bunched her blanket, pillow and wadded hoodie to the best of her ability, but it wasn't enough. As the fog slowly lifted her to consciousness, she'd mapped out her day. Collect herself, eat, get a job, buy a cheap mattress. Once she moved around the room to put on a pot of tea, she felt herself limbering up. This apartment may be empty and musty, but it was all hers.

"I guess this is what being a grownup must be like," she said to no one.

During the next few weeks, Laney went about her job-hunting mission to pay for some furniture, as her savings had shrunk considerably. Grocery shopping was a whole new experience on her budget. Pasta was always cheap. Wieners and beans could go a long way. She was a fast study of the Buy One Get One Free specials. She mournfully eyed some shrimp in the seafood department. She would have to settle for many meals of peanut butter and day old bread. She almost forgot to get paper plates.

Laney's cell phone was the only luxury item her one remaining credit card could cover for a few months, so that was her salvation. Mom surely was worried about her, so Laney felt it was time to call home. She reached the answering machine, so she responded that she was still alive and had found an apartment and would call another time.

Noshing on a peanut butter sandwich and off-brand potato chips, she used the phone to scroll through want ads online. Many of them had seductive wording that promised how one could earn big money fast if they were motivated, excited and willing to work hard. The first few calls sounded like high-pressure sales jobs. Now Laney was learning what to avoid. After four hours, she finally saw something promising: An opening at a custom print shop. She had no experience in printing, but the manager didn't seem to care. They were understaffed. She'd done the fast-food route before so this was a step up. A week later, she was offered the job over the phone.

Laney got her mattress and other items at garage sales and dollar stores. Between the meager print shop wage and her guitar practicing, she didn't get out much. Except the day she finally summoned up the courage to enter the bar below her apartment. It was daylight, so the risk factor was lessened. Shading her head to get a glance through the window, it was as she expected. The patrons were all older men who didn't appear to have anywhere to go. The ones who weren't playing poker or sharing conversation were silently watching the small television attached high on a wall. The bell on the door made a harsh clang, announcing her entrance. Every head turned to see this little lost girl, and all conversation stopped.

"Hi, everybody. I'm a friend of Vic's, okay I'm a tenant upstairs, but I thought I'd stop in to say hi. I don't mean to crash the party, but I thought at least I'd introduce myself after all this time." She was babbling like a teenager.

"If Vic vouches for you, we're good, kid," said a tall, pale man with an Air Force jacket. The ice was broken. One of the men offered her a stool at the bar, which she took as an honor. A man behind the bar introduced himself as Blackie. He looked to be in his fifties with salt-and-pepper hair and beard, the build of a power-lifter, and wearing a black t-shirt that threatened to burst with his every move.

"Care for something?"

Laney never drank at lunchtime, but she sensed it was an unspoken rite of passage here.

"Beer's fine."

Blackie never asked her for ID, a first time for Laney, given her small stature.

"You'll have scotch, with a beer chaser."

Laney never liked the hard stuff. "Really, a beer's fine."

"Then you'll be having the scotch with a beer chaser?"

Laney threw her arms up in surrender.

"Scotch and a beer chaser it is!" The entire bar cheered.

She choked down the scotch, and made a gagging face, which elicited another cheer.

Halfway through her beer, her tongue loosened up and she was now comfortable talking to the men. When asked about her past, she'd mentioned that her dad was a veteran, and everybody opened up in spirited conversation. Blackie treated everyone to a free shot of scotch, in memory of Laney's father. This time she choked back both scotch and the tears that welled up. The next few hours were an alcoholic haze of merriment. The men accepted her, and feeling protective, gave the new kid in town plenty of advice. Some of the conflicting advice accelerated into shouting matches, but Laney took it in stride.

12

The next day at the print shop, a young man named Todd Krupin entered. His highlighted hair was perfectly cropped short, with a slight tuft flipped up. He was a looker, Laney noted. And stylish. He slipped a piece of paper onto the counter. He was ordering a vinyl banner for his uncle's upcoming pre-owned cars sale. In the time it took Laney to work out the specifications and costs, he had charmed her with small talk. They laughed several times until the banter between them became flirty. Laney assured Todd that the banner would be ready by 4 PM tomorrow.

The next day, Todd arrived early to find the banner was ready for him. Aside from the banner, business was slow. Once the bill was settled, he asked Laney if he could show her some great sights in Pittsburgh. She admitted she hadn't made time to know the town well, and was delighted by his offer. Friday at 6 PM he'd pick her up from work. As he left, she finally felt that the move here was a positive step. In the meantime, she had to buy a new blouse, since the shop's employee golf-style shirt was the best piece of clothing she had.

• • •

Todd showed up in a cherry red Mazda Mx-5.

"Some ride! You must'a dropped a lotta guap!"

"It's from my uncle's lot. What's the point of working around cars if you don't get some fringe benefits?"

His smooth and cavalier approach to life was a welcomed contrast to Laney's. Old Laney might have chided him for using his uncle's car, but New Laney was due some thrills after the straight-laced, impoverished existence she'd lived since arriving in her new town. Time for some fun!

13

Rather than staying at home to get a daily haranguing from his mother, Mitch stayed at Cousin Ian's apartment in Millvale. Ian Hurst was a tall, slender man with curly chestnut hair cropped neat. He was thirty-five, but kept in shape enough to pass for younger. Of all of Mitch's many cousins, Ian was the one with whom he'd shared the closest bond. As kids, they passed many hours listening to Beatles songs, playing video games and lots of whiffle ball. Once puberty hit Ian, there was a divide. The younger Mitch began wondering why Ian began playing his music so much louder. Ian's interests transitioned to girls, especially once he got his driver's license—Mitch still wanted to tell fart jokes and play whiffle ball.

In his teens, Ian bought a guitar and eventually a bass. Most of the short-lived bands Ian belonged to already had lead guitarists, so Ian was usually relegated to rhythm guitar or bass. Since his bass abilities were called upon more often than not, Ian decided he would know his chosen weapon inside-out. He bussed tables to save up for better equipment. For a time, between work, music and girls, he didn't have time for his younger cousin. But once people near their thirties, age becomes less of a rift.

•   •   •

"Still doing the rock band thing?" Mitch asked.

"A *lot* of bands, actually. I run sound sometimes for others. Gets me other chances to network. And I'm getting fed up running way stations for bums, who think practice is an excuse to get stoned and dawdle." Ian was always drug-free and Mitch was now off the stuff. Not on moral grounds, per se. Mitch had partied a lot in college, but one particular drug experience had been the last for him. Someone had laced a joint with . . . something. It made him wildly paranoid and terrified that he'd never come down and he'd been sick for days. So ended his experimentation. The worst part was that the joint was given to him by a friend. Who knows what a stranger would give him? To Mitch's credit, he was steadfastly weaning himself off the meds Dr. Shim prescribed, despite the occasional craving. As for Ian, he'd personally witnessed enough will-sapped drug casualties during his college years that it kept him from ever touching the stuff. There was another temporary divide between them: Ian's disapproval during Mitch's drug phase. Mitch and Ian were the counter-counter-culture, it seemed.

"I'm on the verge of burning out. Lot of good musicians out there, but tied up with other bands. Sometimes we get some good stand-ins. I just can't seem to crack the code on how to hold a decent band together. It's becoming to be like a second job, and my day job already tears me down." It was only then that Mitch noticed how Ian's eyes had formed dark rings around them since they last met months ago.

"Playing music is a release that gets me through the week. I tend to think I have this gift for a reason."

"Can I come with? When you play? It'd be like the old days."

"Sure. You can be our roadie, heh-heh."

"I'd love to be your roadie. My asking price is five hundred thousand dollars with six-month reviews plus guaranteed performance bonuses. Six weeks of vacation days."

"I'll meet you halfway. How about . . . nothing? Say, did your doctor give you clearance to lift stuff?"

Mitch nodded a yes, trying to ignore Ian's I.C. Light sitting on the living room table. One more week and he'd be off the meds. Maybe an alcohol/meds combo might take him down the wrong path again, so why chance it?

"I'm gonna hit the hay early. Got to get up early and start restoring three months' worth of lost data and the boss gave me a week deadline."

"What's with the socks on your hands?"

"Oh, to keep the lotion moist when I sleep. Playing bass is murder on my fingers."

"Just use a pick, then."

"Not for me. I'm faster without it and have better control of my tone. My favorite bass players don't use picks. John Paul Jones, Louis Johnson, Geddy Lee, David Pegg, John Glascock . . ."

Mitch had no idea who the last two names were, but if he asked, chances were, they'd be up all night.

"G'night, sleep tight. I'll keep it down."

"G'night." Mitch walked over to the I.C. Light to toss it in the trash. There was still some beer in it and a swig wouldn't hurt, would it? Remembering that bad trip he'd suffered made it easier for him to pour the rest down the sink.

14

Laney's first date with Todd was a thrill ride. The sights were downright amazing. Houses standing atop mountains in the distance. Winding back roads through more lush greenery. Old buildings and industrial neighborhoods remade to attract the non-conformists: New Age restaurants, antique clothing stores, Froyo shops and artist workshops. Todd told her that Andy Warhol grew up in Pittsburgh before moving to New York City. Maybe she'd make that transition one day. Stop, she thought. Today was date night.

Aside from the occasional observational quip, Todd wasn't much of a conversationalist, but had all the answers to Laney's barrage of questions. Although not a physically large man, he carried himself with a confidence that Laney found infectious. Strong and silent type, Laney presumed. He took her to a Greek restaurant off the beaten path with cuisine to die for. She was careful not to pig out on the always-replenished salad, homemade breadsticks and lamb chops. But this was her first real meal in ages. Todd was an expert on wine, and took ten minutes to carefully select the proper color and vintage, after sampling several. He even pronounced the names of the wines properly. Once the choice was selected, Laney finally detected Todd's slight accent, which made him exotic as well.

A perfect first date, the kind you see in movie montages. The night ended with a clear view of the stars. Laney thanked him profusely for a wonderful night as he dropped her off a few blocks from where she actually lived. He was good kisser. The walk home was a giddy one. The next day she was off from work and didn't even look at her guitar. Things finally seemed to be going her way.

15

The reconditioned stove gave out. She rustled around in one of her boxes until she found a small hotplate. She may not have planned everything, but she did her best to prepare for certain situations. The night with Todd had been everything she'd hoped it'd be, and then some. His lifestyle was incongruous to hers. If he eventually wanted to see her place, would he feel disgust or pity? That was a problem for another day. They'd spoken on the phone a few times since the date. Small talk that helped each other unload their problems and cheer up. Nice as Todd was, she didn't want to rush things, and he seemed fine with that.

The bar below her apartment could get rowdy some nights. Usually when someone on TV scored a goal or a homerun or a touchdown. But the bellows were substantially muted. Another testament to the craftsmanship of the bar ceiling and her floor. There was a constant din with bursts that would ebb and flow that Laney not only got used to, but began to subconsciously incorporate into different time-changes she'd never otherwise considered while songwriting. This was exciting. Laney wanted to create ear-splitting music that wasn't sanitized for your protection.

16

Arthur Peters stubbed out his cigar before it was finished. It dissatisfied him greatly, as did everything else lately. The Cuban brands didn't seem to be the way he remembered. In his opinion, the decline began far before the U.S. normalization with Cuba. That was the only original thought he had that day and realizing that, he rubbed his huge, rubbery hands over his face in depression. He had wealth that was recession-free, lived in a mansion and indulged his hobby of collecting foreign cars. Cars he could only drive between April and October. Once this would have been his dream, but his possessions couldn't hide the feeling that he was no more than a glorified stock boy.

A gentle rap on his door freed him from his brooding and he collected himself.

"Come in."

"Mr. Peters, sir, you got a minute?"

"As you can see, I've got nothing but time, Matfey."

"Word is, several buildings in Turnbul are being liquidated. Fast. A package deal for next to nothing. Owner is old, and in a hurry to unload them. Could be a good, quiet spot to store supplies. Rankin Bridge is right there—"

"Matfey, you think so small it pains me."

"I'm very sorry, Mr. Peters. I thought you'd want to know before the government does. They've been eying the area for some time. Probably for some bleeding heart setup, DUI schools, drug treatment centers, social workers."

"The term you're looking for is reutilization. Sometimes, those buildings stay unused if not managed right."

Arthur's eyebrows raised, looking through Matfey. If managed right, this could be a new form of revenue stream. Surely this would impress his bosses enough to rescue him from this internment to a warmer clime.

17

Mitch attended Ian's gigs that took place at various and often bewildering venues. Bars, of course, plus college campuses, bowling alleys, small diners. The diner venues didn't always go so well, since the loud music annoyed the customers. Mitch saw the downside and the benefits. About 2 AM every gig he helped collect the gear that stank of stale beer. But he did enjoy the benefits, sharing intimate moments with strange girls. He'd witnessed the worst shows. One was at a youth correctional center where the literally captive audience clamored for hardcore freestyling beats to burn off energy. A skinhead shoved through the cops and yanked one of Ian's shoes off. The other bad show was at a high school, where the lack of turntable-scratching caused an uproar. One of the band members foolishly ordered the teens to shut up and show some respect. They barely got out with equipment and hides intact. Those nights taught him a lesson. Gave him a game plan: a) research a venue, and b) learn how to read a crowd. Most nights were not as eventful, but Mitch watched Ian in action with fascination, envying the musicianship. In the wee hours when the two would grab some food, Ian, ever the perfectionist, would self-flagellate about his performance.

18

She hadn't felt this way since her first boyfriend in middle school. Laney had the best of both worlds, it seemed. Time with Todd gave her a flush of new vitality, and he gave her space to do her own thing. Vic even had the stove fixed. One day, while she was warming some canned soup, an unsettling thought snapped her out of her reverie. A thought you can't stifle once it takes residence in your brain. When she was at her happiest, her nature was to let her guard down and open herself to mental bear traps. She remembered her exhilaration at nineteen, when she finally could afford a quality amp. That exhilaration dampened the next morning, when her father, Master Sergeant Douglas W. Kilburn died.

She'd accepted this incredible loss surprisingly well. It was most likely stoicism because she thought that's what Dad would have wanted. Time had passed and she never spoke about it, unless Mom needed consoling. Brother Terry was better equipped to help Mom though her periodic crying jags. Laney buried her grief and began to form ways of moving past this loss. At least Dad didn't suffer a long, lingering death. She thought she had closed the door emotionally until that day at Blackie's bar.

•   •   •

Laney heard a bump next door and raced down her stairs, around the back, and up to Margo's.

"You okay in there, Margo?"

"Just a minute," said a soft voice.

More than a minute passed before Margo finally opened the door. She was on her knees, reaching up to open the door. The apartment reeked of dust and piss. Laney fought back her revulsion.

"What happened, Margo?"

"I tripped, but . . . I'm okay, I think. My damn knees give out sometimes."

Laney was engulfed in pangs of shame. Even though Blackie checked on her every day, she should have stopped by before now, but she had been caught up in her own self-interests.

"Help me to my seat. Uh!"

"Maybe you should get out and, y'know, go for a walk. Get your circulation going."

"Blackie tells me that every day and I'm telling you what I told him! I can't make it down those steps, and even if I did, someone your age wouldn't think twice about robbing me!"

There was no retort. How do you mount an argument with someone who'd obviously made up her mind years ago?

"That's right! I watch the news! The streets are crawling with animals! Animals! Preying on the elderly, thinking we're loaded with jewelry. You probably hang out with some of them, with your parties and defacing property for laughs! There's no respect for the elderly anymore and your generation just accepts it and moves on to the latest celebrity gossip!"

Margo was a piece of work. Laney was verbally wind-blown and offered nothing in response. There was no point. It was a new world, for better or worse, and no point in reverse-engineering her. She knew plenty of people half Margo's age set in their ways. She was bent on not being like that. A few decades from now, Laney may very well eat those beliefs, for all she knew. One thing she did know was that Margo's abrasive personality was toxic.

"If you're sure you're alright, Margo, I have some errands to run."

"Fine! At least I have Blackie to check on me! Not like my dirtbag son who disowned me, and my lazy-ass grandkids! Lord, take me!"

Laney left, because Margo had clearly accepted her lot in life, with complaining and television her only pastimes.

19

Arthur now owned the old man's buildings, purchased for a pittance. Arthur made sure there were no other buyers. Arthur had Matfey make arrangements to pay off all the right people. Code enforcement. Union members who kept secrets from their Teamster brethren. Some on-the-take cops. Some who owed Arthur for fixing drunk-driving violations. This group proved useful in making things happen quickly. Now came the tricky part. He intended for the buildings to serve their intended purpose, but first he had to make a big media splash to announce his new role: Philanthropist.

Weeks after his associates laid out a plan to his satisfaction, Arthur decided to hold a press conference at a run-down patch of land in Turnbul. In the guise of respected businessman, he'd perfected the art of pouring on both charm and many drinks while rubbing elbows with people of influence. This included station managers and other news outlets who guaranteed his press conference would make the 6 o'clock news. Arthur had propagandized his event as socially uplifting, to give the media a positive story during a time of bleakness. They welcomed a puff piece to sandwich between house fires, convenience store robberies and international affairs. Best of all, word spread that the noontime event was a catered affair.

Plenty of free food was a good way to soften up any naysayers. A retinue of reporters surrounded the makeshift stage. Some hailed from television, some news radio, prominent bloggers and even the free hipster paper, *Freeloader*. Then came a variety of high-range squeals as Arthur adjusted the microphone on his podium.

"Dear ladies and gentlemen of the press. I come to you, not as a man of means, but as a representative of a family of mere immigrants, coming to American shores from humble beginnings. When the Berlin wall fell, and communism was in its dying days, the opportunity of this country was now available to us. The opportunity only freedom allowed. I was later saddened to see that even in here, there was poverty and many who said this country's best days were behind it. I swore on my mother's deathbed that if I had the means one day, I would remember her kindness and pay it forward. After much rumination, I have purchased these unused buildings and will remake them as monuments of hope. Monuments that will provide the tools necessary for this neighborhood and surrounding townships: family counseling, substance abuse recovery, job training and more, in cooperation with the government. We can begin to bring about poverty alleviation. Provide economic empowerment to the powerless. We must invest in our future. And what is the future I ask?"

The following silence may have been a reaction to the ambiguity of his question, but it hit the right beat for his follow-up statement.

"That's right: our children. The youth of today believe they won't do as well as their parents, but we can show them otherwise."

Just when Arthur's lieutenants prepared to wrap up the conference, per schedule, Arthur continued. He was going off the page as he fell in love with his voice and preached with the stridency of an evangelist.

"And today! I present a challenge to my fellow captains of industry! Follow my lead and donate time, resources and money to help the less fortunate! I'm setting up The Peters Foundation and I cast a light on greedy corporations to donate and re-energize Turnbul to its former glory!"

There was a smattering of applause in the audience, and Arthur did his best to harness the pride of his newfound adulation. There were follow-up questions, but the attending members of the press were hand selected by cronies. This insured that embarrassing queries were nonexistent.

Later, at Arthur's office, Matfey couldn't hide the puzzled look on his face.

"So your revenue increase is a plan to give money away? Maybe I'm missing something."

"We build up this charitable foundation, do one book for us, one for the public. Except *now*, there'll be an endless faucet of money. You should pay attention more. Granted, there's enough paper-pushers to keep the country running, but there are plenty of others who just go through the motions, trust me. Hell, both fed and local agencies approve the most ridiculous grants. Art made of feces, absurd things like that. They got money to piss away. Any politician notices, you barter with them. You'd be surprised how cheap these politicians cost. They want to keep living the good life. Blank checks from Uncle Sam. We create ghost employees. Nobody notices. Goddamn it, I should'a thought of this before."

20

Laney and Todd's relationship continued to blossom. Once she felt comfortable enough, she brought her guitar and amp to his apartment to play some songs she'd written. This was a gargantuan step for her: playing her music for another. Todd really got a kick out of witnessing this side of Laney for the first time. While he failed to grasp many of the nuances and literary references of her lyrics, he did appreciate her talent to an extent. Having a chick rocking a guitar made her hotness level, according to his own personal gauge, rise substantially. He clapped after the last song from her short set. She got affirmation from her first audience of one.

"Next stop, Madison Square Garden," said Laney with a grin.

"That's right. Hey, you like Cuban? There's a killer place down the street . . ."

Laney did her best to shake off the immediate disillusionment that threatened to swallow her whole. Did Todd think of this as just a hobby? Maybe she didn't express how important her music was to her identity. She'd been used to the indifference from old friends she considered uncultured, but was blindsided by Todd's. Maybe she was making too much out of nothing. No sense in processing all this tonight. She was hungry, anyway.

21

Ian was glad to have Mitch stay at his apartment. It became more cramped than he was used to, but not overly so. Mitch travelled light and the couch was good enough for Mitch to sleep on. Ian's day job writing computer code was exhausting, but at least he now had someone to bitch to when he got home. "Bitching with Mitch" they began to call it. When Ian would go on a mad tear about his job dissatisfaction, Mitch was a good listener, something he'd picked up while at the hospital. As an ad man, Mitch had been a force of nature who didn't think twice about cutting other people's comments short with his own ideas. After all, he considered himself the sharpest executive who knew best, or at least he'd thought so then. Clearly Ian's daily displeasure needed release and finding time to perform music was his outlet. If Ian applied all that squandered energy to his music, there'd be no stopping him, Mitch thought. Mitch's situation drove him to quit his job and selfishly hoped the same would happen to Ian. Mitch had been given a second chance and believed he was brought back to life for a purpose. A purpose he needed Ian for, whether Ian suspected it or not. This was not a thought that made him particularly proud, but as a man on borrowed time, Mitch now felt he could move mountains. All he needed were the right people and Ian could be that first plateau.

22

Laney and Todd continued to spend time together, but some of the luster had begun to fade. She had bared enough of her soul to share songs, but gradually built up unspoken resentment that he never asked her about her music. To her, this was no hobby, this was a calling. Given time, maybe he could better understand. Beyond his capricious and outgoing personality, she failed to get a read on his inner thoughts. Was Todd a solitary thinker or simply shallow? Laney gave him a pass. After all, she was guilty of self-absorption, too. It was the main ingredient of her creativity.

After the lukewarm reception Todd gave her, she began playing open mike nights on Mondays and Tuesdays, the nights with the smallest crowds. She never told Todd about it. She needed a boost in confidence, and he'd only be a distraction. Todd's reaction brought back memories of her mom's and Terry's damning faint praise, followed by a "That's nice, dear." She'd feel diminished, like a child doing a dance at the dinner table. Like her friends in Maryland, it was seen only as cute, despite her insistence that music would be her career. Moving away may have been tough sledding, but she could now reinvent herself.

•   •   •

Also, Todd never asked about seeing Laney's place. Part of it was lack of desire to go to that part of town. He was a high-roller whose job description was cryptic. One view of her home could not auger well. But it'd have to happen eventually, no?

23

At 6:45 PM, Ian slammed the door to his apartment hard, his face a mosaic of anger, hysteria and hopelessness. Mitch couldn't even get in a "hello" before Ian darted to the refrigerator. Ian popped the top of a beer then spun on his heel to face Mitch.

"Layoffs for over half the department today . . . and now it's on me to take on their load! On top of my own! What do they expect of me? I swear, James is supposed to be the department head, but he doesn't know dick about writing code! He does everything by rote, asks me the hard questions, and takes credit for everything!"

Ian plopped his ass next to Mitch's on the couch. Ian had a thousand-mile stare, cradling his beer without having taken a sip. Mitch knew it was time to say nothing, just listen.

"I don't know what to do. I just don't know. I've been an insomniac for the past few months. I'm sure you've heard me milling about in the kitchen at all hours. This job is going to kill me. And the market's not good right now to look elsewhere."

The two of them sat quietly for ten minutes. The only signs of life were Ian's sighs and all the postures associated with restless seething. Mitch, feeling uncomfortable, began drafting opening lines in his head to dispel the tension. None of them would work, he decided, so he sat there at his cousin's side, waiting for him to talk first. Ian's beer assumed room temperature, untouched.

"I'm fenced in," said Ian, breaking the silence.

24

Todd and Laney sat at a table in a local coffee shop, wordlessly texting to others. Tedium had taken hold and it required increased effort to make this relationship work. Laney wasn't the quitting type. At least until a situation became hopeless.

"You know what'd I'd like to do? Check out some new supplies at that Guitar Glow shop we passed on our way here." Her fingers clasped the cuffs of her sleeves in excitement as she put on amorous eyes for him. She did that from time to time to attempt to regain the spark they once had.

"Sure. Whatever you want."

At Guitar Glow, Todd milled about, killing time on his phone, while Laney spoke to the guitar associate, Michael, about arcane models and makes of instruments. Once in a while, she heard Todd whisper angrily and unintelligibly—probably pig-Latin—about her. Then his mood would change, yakking it up merrily, minutes later. It was distracting, but she shut him out so she could wrangle as much information this guitar associate volunteered. She could tell Todd was subtly urging her to hurry up, so she did her best to ignore him. Maybe Todd was jealous, and if that was a burr in his ass as payback, so be it.

After a half hour, Todd made some malcontented noises, strongly suggesting he was ready to leave.

"What say we grab whatever you want, then head over to

the casino? Some of my friends will be there and you could meet them."

Laney was leaning towards shallow in her judgment of Todd. He seemed oblivious that she was enjoying the impromptu guitar tutelage.

"Hey, thanks for spending so much time with me, Michael. I'll be back sometime. This was very educational. I'll take these boxes of strings," she told him.

"It's on me," Todd said as he leaned over Laney's shoulder with his credit card.

Her feelings ran hot and cold with him with more frequency lately.

At the casino, Laney felt out of place. She was more comfortable in darkened rooms that invoked mystic qualities than all these gaudy lights that allowed no shadows to be cast.

Upon meeting Todd's friends, Laney quickly assessed his friends as dullards who brought out a thuggish, jock mentality in him. She felt like an accessory and couldn't get a word in when "the bros" waxed ineloquent about the past.

Laney began making the rounds of the local music scene, sometimes with Todd, sometimes without. Todd thought he'd score some points by indulging her. She'd introduce herself to bands and pick their brains while Todd would check out other girls. Some of the musicians were helpful, some found her annoying with her endless questions. More than a few male performers fed her stories simply for the intent of sleeping with her. Once she sensed that, she'd tell them she was in a relationship, threadbare as it was. She was no groupie hunting for sexual favors. She was culling information on band dynamics. The musician who was the most generous with his experiences was veteran musician Ian Hurst.

•   •   •

On a Thursday evening, Laney's online guitar lesson was interrupted by her ringtone.

"Hey, Todd! How's it goin'? What? This weekend? I can't! You didn't say . . . look, I'm cocooning all weekend. I really need time to polish off some songs. I'm seeing a band next week and—"

Her phone glared Call Ended in red.

Todd had made reservations at his father's cottage in an isolated part of Lake Erie. He assumed that Laney would be excited. All of his other girls did. Emma really loved the place. He called her up to see what she was doing this weekend.

Laney was saddened but it hadn't eroded her determination. Creature comforts were few but she couldn't give in to them or she'd lose her edge. Watching *Glengarry Glen Ross* at a young age left quite an impression on her: "Coffee's for closers only."

25

Over time Laney and Todd's relationship continued to sour. Their respective ideas on how to best spend free time was worlds apart. Initially, they had an understanding that they wouldn't smother each other. But Todd began to sound clingy, exasperated that she would turn down his elaborate, not to mention, expensive plans. Rather than a coercion, it was a turnoff.

After many weeks of hot-and-cold times with Todd, Laney thought to put all doubts to rest once and for all. It was time he finally got to see her apartment. He surprised her by agreeing, intrigued at the prospect. The following day, she had made a painstaking effort to tidy up what she jokingly called her little shanty. She even prepared Cajun stew, a special recipe of Nana Kilburn's, reserved only for special occasions.

When he finally did show up, his expression was less-than-pleasant.

"Wow. This is . . . different."

Todd's lifestyle was high-end, but surely he could appreciate the homey touches she had given the place. She was hardly a bum and took pride in what was hers.

She poured on the congeniality to better acclimate Todd, but it was obvious he'd rather be elsewhere. He went through the motions. He complimented her on the smell of the stew, and enjoyed the taste. However, it was clear as day that he was uncomfortable, the way the lord of a manor would be eating among servants.

"Last night, I learned something new on the guitar. Honestly, I don't know how people got things done before the internet. I'll show you after we eat."

"You're the only girl I know who's spends so much time on her hobby."

Laney stopped halfway through her meal, her appetite gone.

"Well . . . it means a lot to me," she squeaked out softly. She then washed dishes while Todd checked his text messages, with no offer to assist her.

When she finished, he had migrated over to her couch, still texting. She grabbed her guitar and sat on a folding chair, rather than next to him. She was in a foul mood and couldn't unlock herself from it. She tinkered with her guitar, almost as a test. Todd never looked up from his phone.

His laissez faire approach to life, once charming, was now an irritant. Even his random musings began to sound like a fish tank full of stupid.

"I'd like to, like, adopt a kid one day. Too many people on this planet, I think. I got what it takes to raise a child, right?" Todd was better suited to adopt a highway.

After all the evidence was presented, she concluded that Todd was a shallow boor after all. The glossy coat of paint he once shared with the Mazda they rode on their first date had worn down to the primer. Laney struggled with compartmentalizing a relationship with musical exploration. Some artists could, but she found it counter-productive. Laney didn't come to Pittsburgh to land a boyfriend, after all.

He stayed glued to his phone, which now was clearly a distraction from the trappings of Laney's apartment.

"That is annoying," Todd said under his breath.

"What's annoying?" she said at him, stone-faced. He thought she hadn't heard him and now he acted like he'd been busted by a school teacher. He'd had enough.

"You. Playing the same shit over and over. Driving me up the fucking wall. In fact, I just texted a few friends about you."

"At least I have plans for my life. What craft are you honing, by the way? How many words you can text a minute?"

"Hey, hey, dial it back a bit, baby. Maybe I don't like competing with an idiotic guitar for your attention. I have options, and I don't appreciate you blowing me off when we could be enjoying ourselves."

"You'll never understand. Music is one of the ways I enjoy myself. I can't just drop what I'm doing to spend the weekend in Erie. I'm young, I have a lot of time to fall on my face, but in the meantime, if I give up on my music, I'll be stuck at the print shop forever."

"My music, my music," Todd said, imitating her voice. He added, "You sound so fucking gay when you say that."

Laney could no longer hold in the combustion she'd built up.

"You . . . ass . . . hole. You will live and die a total fucking slacker and will have made no impact in the world when you're gone. You're a petulant child when you don't get your way. Not to mention your cruel streak. Tell me, what did you think was so great about The Hotseat that you needed to share it with me? Keep me in line? Crush my dreams? It certainly seemed that dream crushing was as fun for you as it was for the rest of those morons. At least those performers had the balls to get up on stage. They had ambition! You, on the other hand, are a lazy bastard who acts all independent when your family's probably paying the bills! You wouldn't last a week on your own!"

"Who in the fuck do you think you're talking to? I can do a lot better than you!" he said as he stood up. "You can rot in this garbage dump for all I care!" He charged out of the apartment, storming down the steps without closing the door.

26

Donations began pouring in. Substantial endowments from private companies, the detached affluent who tossed money at the world's ills, and stop-light cash collections from the Joe Six-packs. All low-hanging fruit for the Peters Foundation. The smaller, underfunded charities who piggy-backed with the foundation now found themselves with surpluses to allocate. In record time, Arthur deposited a substantial amount of money to his Swiss bank account. All in the name of philanthropy. Arthur's new public role gave him that tingle he hadn't known since the Bratva promoted him to Kassir. Months ago, he knew only despair, thinking he'd peaked on his various and sundry enterprises. His biggest disappointment was not getting a piece of the Rivers Casino. But that was now just water under the bridge. He was now a local star and liked that feeling. The icing on the cake was that he would be celebrated as he laundered more money. His business was not only recession free, but a substantial portion of these fronts now qualified for tax-exempt status. He'd established enough buffers in the chain of bureaucracy to keep the inquisitive busy with years of red tape.

From the moment his words were broadcast, he was a star and he liked that feeling. He didn't want his newfound grandeur to drift away as the media moved onward to one late-breaking disaster after another.

If he played up his public portrayal of benevolence, he

could draw in even more new revenue streams.

The clubs he owned pretty much ran themselves. They paled compared to this new Ponzi scheme. If he kept receiving more capital from high-minded business and government associates, the possibilities of his empire's expansion were endless.

He was already eyeing his next target for reutilization: Tungsten Heights. Its population had dwindled the past two decades. The fast food chains and grocery stores had long been closed and boarded up. Package stores and gas stations remained busy, doing service through revolving bullet-proof glass. The only noteworthy business was a dilapidated bar called The Silverfish, one of those clubs that you had to ask directions to at least three times before you found it. Its main attractions were half-time all-you-can-eat Buffalo wing night, happy hour and the occasional cover band. It was the only night life this shell of a town still retained. Its owner, Jerry DeSantis, swore, more out of stubbornness than logic, he'd be the last man standing in Tungsten Heights. Arthur had his driver drive by and saw the resemblance to a post-apocalypse nightmare. But The Silverfish could be prime real estate, once it was leveled with the whole block to create a main access road to Upper Merrill, with its well-to-do neighborhoods. Tungsten Heights could be a gateway, drawing in a better class of people.

He'd contact his nephew, Todd. He wasn't good for much, but he knew how to have a good time and knew what was in vogue. Todd wasn't on speaking terms with Arthur's adult children. Considered the runt of the litter, Todd had been intimidated by their incessant drive to be well ensconced in the family business. Todd usually took the path of least resistance, as his parents reminded him on a daily basis. But this was his shot. He could make over Tungsten Heights as a new hotspot, and a beacon of job creation of the fanciful kind. Todd and his fellow hipsters could shed some light on how to make Tungsten Heights a happening place, complete with businesses targeting the youth market. Art galleries. Bistros. Cultural centers. Coffee and pastry shops. Pizza places coated with haphazard painting done in chic hippy-art and phrases. Even a coin-operated Laundromat for the starving artists. It could be a way for Todd and his uncle to bond.

27

At Marshall's Amp, a low-lit, small nightclub, Ian and his patchwork band wrapped up the first half of their set for the sixteen patrons who applauded out of politeness more than admiration. Relieved, Ian placed his bass on its stand. Then, spotting the new girl in town, he could feel his meh melt away when he got off the stage.

"Good set, Ian. Well, you were good anyway."

Ian lolled his head, displaying his exasperation in comical fashion. "Thanks . . . Laney, isn't it? This is my cousin Mitch. He's crashing with me for a while."

"Hey there, Laney."

"Hey, Mitch! How do?"

Mitch and Ian grew to adore Laney when they made the rock club rounds. Not only was she cute, but she could hang with the guys and talk music.

"Whew, it's warm in here." She lifted her hair, fanning her neck to cool off. A casual feminine move Mitch and Ian found quite mesmerizing.

Laney made a three-finger sign to the waitress across the room. Message received.

"You look like you needed that break, Ian."

"Shit, I need a new band!"

"I told you I write songs, right? And I followed your advice on improving my guitar playing, too. Do you give lessons?"

"I don't know. Wrangling these jagoffs while hustling for

venues takes a lot out of me. It. Sucks."

Three longneck I.C. Lights plonked down on their table.

"Put it on my tab," Ian said to the waitress.

The three clinked the bottle necks together in salute.

"Up your ass," Mitch said.

"Up your ass," Ian said.

"Up your ass," Laney added, having no idea what that meant.

After a long swig, the trio chuckled, then Laney's demeanor quickly morphed back into seriousness.

"Well . . . I sold my car and saved some cash from the sign shop job before I quit. Because it's not why I moved to the 'Burgh. I figure if I live frugally, I can get by for a year. I really want to make a go at making it in the music scene. This may be a big mistake, but I won't know unless I try. I think I have what it takes, but I'd love to build a good band from the ground up. I know I'm being presumptuous, but maybe you can show me the ropes during one of your gigs."

An exhausted Ian found it refreshing to hear a musician with a fire in her belly. She reminded him of what he was, years ago. So much vigor.

"Sure, why not?"

"I promise I won't get in your way and I'll do whatever it takes to learn from you. I'll carry equipment, call me your intern, whatever."

Ian raised an eyebrow as Mitch did his. In Ian's music circle, Laney had been labelled bitchy, but he saw her as canny and determined. Something sorely missing with his current bandmates.

"Huh. I recently quit my job too, for different reasons," Mitch said. "But I haven't figured out what my next step will be. Can't play a note, but I religiously devour rock music, new and old, rockumentaries, podcasts, since I was a kid. Hanging around Ian taught me a lot about musical nuances and influences, good times. I still follow up all the new trends, hoping that something will reignite the mainstream music landscape. Rock bands need to be household names again."

Ian remained silent, the wheels turning in his mind. Maybe, he mused, he had cracked the code.

"I'm in my mid-thirties. I've been around the music scene quite a while, and by bad timing, or misfortune, I've missed out on joining more successful bands. Sure, I pitch in here and there, but I'm not going to be that middle-age jagoff who plays bad ballads at weddings. I've had many sleepless nights wondering if it's not over for me. Let's see what you've got some time, who knows? Can't be worse than playing babysitter." Immediately after Ian's comment, he saw one of the babysat from across the room, saluting him with a beer, which Ian reciprocated.

"Yeah, big ups to you too, jaggoff," Ian wisecracked.

"Look, I'm hard-working and quick to learn . . . at least, according to my last review at the print shop," she said, smirking while tying her hair back in a ponytail.

"I think you're on the same page," Mitch noted.

"My boyfriend and I just broke up so I've sworn off dating for a while. What I absolutely *don't* need are distractions. If you like what you hear, maybe we can make stuff happen. But we need someone to handle the mundane stuff."

Mitch saw his opening and chimed in.

"Someone to deal with finances, bookings, promotion, etcetera. Essentially take the weight off your backs so you can focus. Something like that?"

"I'm thinking manager, maybe. The hard part is finding someone reliable for no money," Laney said.

Ian emptied his beer, looked at Mitch, then looked at Laney. Ian, mildly buzzed by a beer guzzled on an empty stomach, made a suggestion borne of desperation.

"If you're that serious—I mean it—I think *Mitch* could be your manager-slash-talent agent."

Laney looked at Mitch quizzically. Mitch's face froze, as

if he just learned he was three-quarters Martian. Laney kept staring at Mitch, silently evaluating.

"Mitch would take a bullet for me. He's a total pro. He may look goofy, but has a good head on his shoulders."

"Thank you so very much, Ian."

"Look, Laney, I've been in a holding pattern. If you're halfway decent, and are open to some advanced lessons, who knows? I'm a beaten man."

"Are you just saying that, Mitch, this guy sitting right here, is qualified because he's your cuz?"

"I just quit a good-paying job at an advertising agency. My job required decisiveness, mapping out projects weeks in advance, dealing with freelance talent, book balancing. I know a metric fuck-ton of the business end of rock history. Who made money, who got screwed. I also study current business models in music, because it fascinates me. Totally in my wheelhouse."

"Um," said Laney with her forefinger propping up her lower lip. "Ummm, okay, Hmmm . . . here we go, brainiac . . . lessee, ever hear of The Wrecking Crew?"

"Oh, yeah. A group of LA session musicians who played backup for everybody during the '60s. They really weren't a band, but that was what the session drummer, Hal something . . ." Mitch closed his eyes and snapped his fingers a few times. "Black . . . no . . . Blaine called them and it stuck." Mitch folded his arms as he beamed with no small amount of cockiness.

"Managerial experience and you know your stuff? Look at you."

"Music trivia is fine and dandy," said Ian, "but I think you know there will be a lot of pressure on us. I've got a lot of experience to share, so I need to be the Henry Higgins to your Eliza Doolittle."

This was a gift from the gods for Laney. Somehow, tonight, a connection was made, an earnestness, the kind you can't force.

She had to clear something up before she got her hopes too high.

"But . . . you're related. How do I know you won't circle the wagons, having *me* working for both of you?"

"Hey, you said you'd do anything, like moving equipment, interning, remember?" Ian said. "I don't even know your skill level. Let's not put the cart before the horse."

"Yeah, yeah, you're right. I'll gut it out, like my father used to say."

"What you just said, Laney, means you're halfway there."

"So if this is ground zero for the greatest band of the ages, how do we ensure no one gets screwed?"

Mitch cupped his hands on the table as he presented his offer.

"I'll make a contract and get it notarized. Even split. Any legalese either of you don't understand, I'll break it down for you. If you don't get paid, I don't get paid. So it'll be in my best interest that you get better-paying gigs."

"Mitch could be a tie-breaker on decisions if needed," said Ian.

"Let me mull it over for a while," Laney said.

"I'm not saying tonight, Laney, but if all goes well, we could try a . . . *Mitch-ocracy* and see how that goes," Ian said.

Laney showed no signs of disagreement.

"Okay." Mitch wanted to jump up and shout expletives of joy, but that might've killed the deal.

"Waitress! Please bring me and my fellow travelers a second round!" Mitch loudly barked to expend his pent-up energy.

28

This heady meeting of minds at Marshall's Amps could very well have dissolved when real-world routines resumed the next day. All the big talk could have faded into fantasy, had Ian not called her that afternoon. The first time they met at his apartment to play music, it was clear that she was no poser. After a long day of playing, with only one break for Chinese delivery, he saw a lot of promise in Laney. Not necessarily in playing ability, but willpower. A fresh face, unhampered by ennui. She wanted this bad. Her songs, at parts, were genuinely moving and solid. And, more importantly, had very catchy hooks.

Over the course of a month, Ian gave her a crash course on how to better know the wide variety of sounds a guitar could elicit. Smearing. Sustain. The finger-tapping style preferred by metal bands. She would be best utilized as a rhythm guitarist for now, but he wanted her to understand these techniques in case she came up with new song ideas. He had a collection of guitars for various needs and was a font of knowledge of many instruments, including the voice of each. Its tone and timbre as well as when to add various grace notes, intervals, lower fourths. Things listeners took for granted when hearing their favorite song. She felt overwhelmed, but did her best to keep up with this flood of information. At times their emotions ran the gamut from elation to vexation. Nonetheless, he was pleased to see her learning more quickly than expected.

She even took basic lessons in bass. If things worked out, it would free up Ian to play lead at times. Many lessons later, she admitted she wasn't keen about getting too caught up in precision. She may have been a pup, but she ultimately knew what she wanted: To learn the ropes, while maintaining the value of imperfection. By all counts, Keith Moon was a sloppy drummer, unfit for any type of music save rock 'n' roll. And he was a sloppy genius on the drums. Ian agreed that may be the best way to go. He loved King Crimson's Robert Fripp but he also loved The Ramones. While the student hadn't exceeded the master, she began to surprise him with new musical suggestions. It was as if they'd known each other in past lives. Their musical cohesion was actually working. Laney didn't have to pull intern duties after all—such a silly thought to have blurted out. Any food runs or lifting equipment would be done as a full-time band member. Ian was so energized, he cashed in all his remaining vacation days from work. He felt more alive than he had in years. He had Mitch put the call out for auditions.

Mitch arranged the auditions through all forms of social media and even took out an ad in *Freeloader*. *Drummer and a lead guitarist needed. No posers.* They all met at a friends' storage facility. Laney's rhythm guitar and Ian's bass were anchors in need of ambitious barnacles. The Mitch-ocracy, as promised, was the tie-breaker during disputes over potential band members. Members of Ian's previous bands showed up, which made the auditions more uncomfortable than expected. Over four days of tedious pruning, the new band members were finally anointed. The drummer, Steve Wilkinson was 6'5" with long, dark, greased-back hair. His teeth were a mess, but who'd notice, since he'd be sitting in the back? Paul Varlotta, sporting a slight beer-gut, a knit cap and a mustache, stepped up to play some lead. At first, he appeared to be the nervous sort but when he closed his eyes to focus, he felt his way around some well-known solos and was tight. Ian felt he could draw out more fireworks from him over time. Neither men could be accused of being masters of their instruments, but it was obvious they were hungry and tried the hardest. Steve and Paul were told the first actual band meeting would take place in a week, provided Paul lost the 'stache.

29

Arthur met with more politicians and businessmen, most of whom were swayed by Arthur's charisma. Ask them what they did for a living and they'd never shut up. Best way to glean more information than they'd realize. Especially after they had a few highballs in them. As the new reutilization deal had progressed, his well-to-do partners embraced the positive news coverage. Arthur's plans were as audacious as they were infectious. He was quite the charmer, contriving conversations so these new power-brokers came to the conclusions he wanted. This gave him another rush, like a compulsive gambler. They assisted him in speeding up his timeline.

30

One night at Ian's apartment, he and Mitch watched a movie someone had recommended. It was crap. Halfway through, they grew bored as the story hit the same formulaic beats. Ian skipped the Hitchcock marathon for this? But he took joy in Mitch's snide commentary. It reminded him of when they were kids and cracked each other up. Ian found the incidental music to be pedestrian and a soft target to pick apart. The laughable attempts at creating suspense or romance. The music sounded comically inappropriate, as if the score was written without seeing the movie. This action movie devolved to a comedy, probably not the filmmaker's intent. It was so bad, it was a perfect thing, and they couldn't stop watching it. The final scene showed yet another hero-dangling-from-a-cat-walk-over-a-raging-fire. Mitch prepared to shut off the DVR, but Ian waved him off.

"I have got to learn who's responsible for the music. That was too damn goofy."

As the credits rolled, Ian made a gasp that threatened to vacuum all small objects in the room.

"Tommy Norris! Tommy fucking Norris! Can't friggin' believe it!" Before Mitch queried what a Tommy Norris was, Ian turned to him with squinty eyes and a gaping smile. Ian said, "He lives here! I've played with him! And he sucks!"

"Okay, he sucks. And?"

"The bar has officially been lowered! If a modest talent

like him can get keyed into making money on music . . ." Ian dashed across the room to get his cell phone.

"Laney!"

"Mmmm'low? Tha' you, een? I'ss pass . . . two-thirdy. Are you drunk?"

"No no! But we *have* to have a band meeting soon as possible!"

"Cannit wait until tomorrow?"

"Sure! Whenever Steve and Paul can make it! Screw it, I'm taking a sick day!"

"Goody goody. C'n I go back t'sleep now?"

"Sure, sure." Laney hung up before Ian could say goodbye. But nothing short of a hurricane could quell Ian's excitement.

"Mitch, hear me out on this . . . ."

31

The following day, Laney woke up with a headache due to lack of sleep. Ian had her so cranked up she'd stared at the ceiling for hours before the racing thoughts left her. She woke later than she'd planned. No time for a shower. She switched off the stale clothes she slept in. A quick sniff of the armpits seemed to check out okay. As luck would have it, Steve happened to be off from his delivery job and Paul worked second shift. So Ian planned the band's lunchtime meeting in a gazebo at the 13th Street Marina. Ian bought enough hoagies and pop for everyone. It was the ideal place to formally introduce Mitch and announce the band's mission statement.

Mitch stood apart from the band, where he could hold court.

"Hey, Steve, hey, Paul. You were probably wondering why we're here. As you know, my name is Mitch Slater. I've been appointed manager by the two-headed hydra that is Laney and Ian."

"What about it?" Steve said before engulfing a piece of hoagie.

"If you're game, what I'm about to say will affect each and every one of us."

Paul, his mustache now growing into the beginning of a

Van Dyke, silently plucked pickles out of his hoagie.

"Jee-zus! Is this what it's about? Y'all brought me here on my day off so this cocksucker can showboat?"

"Steve, Mitch has the floor. Hear him out," Ian said.

"You done, Steve? Because Cocksucker isn't. 'Kay?" Mitch said.

"Laney quit her day job. I've quit my job. As of this morning, Ian turned in his notice. This band may have just been cobbled, but pieces are falling into place. This is as good a time as any to let you know that we are settling for nothing short of nation-wide success. You want in on this, you're in full time. Did The Black Keys worry about holes in their resumes?" His voice built with every proclamation. He'd sold ad space for a living, and considered this a cakewalk by comparison.

"No plan B, dudes! If we all step up, when your sole source of income is music, things'll happen. I'm talkin' performing and eventually, recording great music! The question you have to ask yourselves is, in this age of endless entertainment options, do you have the tenacity and stage presence to stir a crowd enough to bring their asses out on a cold wet wintery day, cramming themselves into a club the size of a port-a-potty to pay for watered-down drinks? I think you all can. I've already planted seeds in the local press, hyping a band that hasn't even played yet. You think I want to publicly look like a fool? That's fucking faith! And you all need to have faith in yourselves! There's no better time to pull the trigger than now. Steve, you gonna drive a delivery truck the rest of your life? And Paul, whatever you do for a living, you think you won't regret not using your musical ability when you're old and too arthritic to plink a string?"

"What's in it for you?" Steve said.

"Maybe I'm naïve enough to believe that rock 'n' roll deserves to be saved! Naïve to believe you all have the potential to bring back serious larger-than-life, ass-kicking, ear-bleeding rock music that will set their audience's asshole hairs on fire!"

Paul nervously increased the pace of his hoagie gnawing.

"And you think we're naïve enough to let you make money off *our* music?"

"Take a look around, and you'll see that I'm the only outsider who gives a healthy shit about making this happen! Ian and I have pooled our resources to get the band buoyed for a few months, tops. Not a lot of money, but an investment to make things happen."

Mitch pointed westward, his face contorted to an open snarl.

"Trust me, I can make more right now as a fucking barista down the road!

"With a small pittance you'll start off making, you'd be impossibly goddam lucky to be rich and famous and I happen to swindle only a couple million from you!

"But I swear on Lemmy's mole, as your manager, I will bust my balls night and day to get you recognition by every means imaginable if you want it bad enough!

"Another thing: No serious romances! If you have a significant other, hand them that 'if you love someone set them free' bullshit. Discounting the occasional groupie who wants a drunken coupling, for all intents and purposes, you are now widows! All eyes on the prize! Lots of touring and online branding! The world is waiting for that Kurt Cobain moment when blaring guitars once again invigorate music across the landscape! When that moment happens, you have to make them want more, demand more of what you've got!"

Laney and Ian looked at each other, trying to keep straight faces.

"I'm recently divorced so that's no issue for me," Paul said sheepishly while adjusting his baseball cap.

Steve was annoyed. He hadn't joined under these conditions.

"Are we done? Meeting adjourned? Or do I need a hall pass?"

"I think I've said all that needs to be said."

"Good!" Steve stormed out of the gazebo, purposely brushing shoulders with Mitch. As his figure and curses faded in the distance, Steve kicked a recycle bin over then threw his can of pop in some overgrown weeds.

Ian placed an assuring hand on Mitch's shoulder.

"Don't sweat it. Where's he gonna go? Really? He's not going anywhere."

Paul's slumped shoulders suggested acquiescence. "A'right, I'm in. By the way, what's a Lemmy?"

32

That night Laney walked around her apartment barefoot, admiring the cheap furniture she'd bought, until her heel jabbed an exposed floorboard nail. She winced quietly, for Margo's sake. Then she angrily wrenched the nail out of the floor. Then she walked to the corner where her guitar leaned, and cradled it in her hands. Using the nail, she forcefully scratched "The Demands" on its body, below the bridge. The nail-scrawling looked crude, as if a maniac had defaced it. Lots of great bands had a "The" in their names. She started the band, it was her right to name it.

33

Arthur and his administrative assistant/mistress were ironing out his arrangements for Tungsten Heights on his computer. The timetable for his reutilization presentation was only months away.

The phone disrupted his concentration. It was Bishop Alexie from the Saint Michael's Russian Orthodox Church. Arthur had gotten to know the bishop quite well, mostly during funerals.

"Artur, I hope you are well, my son."

"Never better, Bishop."

"We have witnessed the kindness you have shown those in need through the television recently, and God blesses you for your benevolence. We at the church would like to contribute some money we had collected from parishioners. God has blessed me by delivering me from a cruel fate others had suffered in my native Ukraine."

Arthur was troubled by this phone call. Bilking deep-pocketed peers and officeholders was one thing, but Arthur's mother was a staunch Catholic. While she turned a blind eye to many things Arthur did, she would be greatly disappointed if he'd willingly taken money from a bishop.

Perhaps if he built a new church in Tungsten Heights, Arthur's sins could be washed away. Arthur didn't like these sort of conundrums. Since making Kassir, he hadn't considered his morality in the afterlife.

"Bishop, I'm in the midst of something right now, and if you forgive me, I must attend to it right away."

"But of course, my son."

Once the phone conversation ended, Arthur felt an emotional upheaval he thought no longer possible. He needed to be alone. He'd had his guards escort his mistress out of the building with a gallantry reserved for royalty. Right now, his private stock of whiskey could drown out, if not wash away, his sinfulness. It had been many years since he was a practicing Catholic. In fact, the moment his mother passed, he blamed God for taking her away so soon and angrily renounced his faith. Somewhere in the recesses of his mind, today, he learned he hadn't entirely buried it.

34

Ian and Laney continued to play, occasionally having spats that turned into yelling matches. The stakes were higher now. She'd become steadfast about how her songs should go, even when Ian insisted she couldn't fully articulate her needs. During one of their practice breaks, Laney paced around in another room, moping. Ian checked his texts as a means of lowering his blood pressure.

It was during this break when Laney had a revelation. The barriers she'd created to protect herself were also inhibiting her. In this case, she was still pushing Ian away from messing with her songs, as they were too personal to her. Either she could stay that teenager who played music to herself in her bedroom, or she could chip away at that barrier and learn more than just technique from Ian. This thought made her queasy like asking to hook up on a date. Songwriting with a partner could be as intimate a relationship as a marriage. She chewed at a cuticle as she swayed back and forth, externalizing her inner struggle. A few minutes later, she re-entered the room to resume practice.

"Ian."

Ian shut down his phone so he could give her his full attention. She felt like she was watching herself in a movie where someone enters a room wearing only a bathrobe before dropping it. Despite the hardships experienced since moving away from home, this was tougher than anything, even breaking up with Todd.

"I can't do this alone, and put on this tortured artist front. I tried it and I have to admit it's not working. This is hard for me to say, but—"

Ian girded himself for the worst.

"—I need you as a writing partner. We put in a lot of hours together, and we've almost been able to read each other's minds. The only thing holding me back is me."

"Glad you said it so I didn't have to. Now let's get back to work," said Ian. Now that the drama had played out, they did just that.

35

Days later, Laney, Ian, Steve and Paul started the first sessions as a band, at the same self-storage unit. Once again, Paul wore a different hat, this time a colorful knit beanie that draped over his ears. Paul's hats were his thing. Steve's hair was now combed forward and long, hiding his face. The back of his head was shaved clean. He'd been hiding the long hair from his delivering days. Company policy included not scaring the customers at their doorsteps.

They started with a few well-known covers to get this neophyte group to gel. Rather than confirming her worst fears, this new collaboration with Ian was a weight off her shoulders. The way one loses a grudge. It was out of her comfort zone and that's where she thrived. Hours passed while they clunked about, feeling out each other's instincts, ferreting out parts that weren't working.

"Ian, I think this is going well, don't you?" she said.

"Sure. Once we tighten up more."

"I could use a pop," Paul said.

"You could use a little less pop, you ask me," Steve wheezed.

Paul chose to ignore him while ambling to the cooler.

Laney changed the subject. "I have something to run by you guys. In my head, the songs are getting better, but they're missing something. I can sing while playing, but I'd need someone to spell me to rest my voice. No offense, Ian, you're great with the harmonies, but I'm thinking lead singer, someone with a harsh growl."

"Whatever," Ian said.

The guys all looked at each other. The thought of splitting gig money even more was as appealing as finding a wet Band-Aid in a salad.

36

Mitch once again did his talent search through the usual forms of media. He was getting better at casting a wider net.

Seeking male lead singer for hard rock band. Vocals should be gritty, more attitude than precision.

When the date arrived, Mitch and The Demands judged several dozen hopefuls. Per Laney's strong suggestions, males showed up, but a few females came to brave the test. Even if one of the girls had a husky, Amy Winehouse style, Laney would have to reexamine the dynamics. For years, Laney romanticized about being her generation's Chrissie Hynde, the female leader. To her relief, none of the girls came close to Winehouse.

Many of the would-be singers were obvious devotees of prime time singing-contest television shows. They could hold a note, mimic other's singing style well, but had no identity of their own. Laney groaned under her breath, disguising her disdain for such shows that took the balls out of popular music.

Then a tall man forcefully brushed his way past the remaining hopefuls. His physique was thin with strong definition, seen through his opened goldenrod button-down shirt. His dark hair was a bird's nest. His leather pants had the belt area cut off, and they threatened to fall off any moment. His face, rugged and misshapen, only added to his animal magnetism. In short, he was genetically engineered to be a rock god.

"Fuck this shit! I got places to be! Got a song I c'n recognize?"

Ian wordlessly mouthed "Honky Tonk Woman" to Paul. The opening guitar chords kicked in. By the third note, this cocksure man seamlessly slinked to the music. In a whiskey-soaked voice, he belted out loud in full-Jagger mode, adding his own touches that were as natural to him as breathing. He appeared to have no bone structure as he snaked about. Upon the song's final crash, everyone in the room knew he was the choice. Most of the remaining wannabes had left by mid-song, knowing they couldn't compete. There was no denying he had presence. They had to lock him in before someone else did.

"Damn."

"Whooo."

"I second that damn!"

"Greg Burdette, nice ta meetcha!"

"I'm Laney. Nice to meet you too. I think I can speak for the band and say you're the guy. Am I right?" The others nodded as one.

"You really knocked it out of the ballpark, Greg. I know you gotta leave, so let us know when you can come to next practice."

"Ah, I just made that shit up. If I had to hear another one of those twats warble, I swear I'd blow my brains out," Greg said as his face shone, illuminated by the struck matchstick that lit his cigarette.

Rock God indeed.

Mitch walked up to Greg, pulling a business card out of his wallet.

"Here's how you reach us. I'm Mitch, their manager."

Greg gave the card a cursory glance before stuffing it in his pants. Not his pockets. His crotch area.

"I'll find them, Mr. Kincaid. Don't know exactly what a manager can do with these ragamuffins, but I choose to go through them and not you, if'n you don't mind." Greg sucked a long drag on his cigarette until it was done. "I'll be stayin' at my lady's place, a few blocks from here. Keller Avenue, next to the Indian restaurant."

Steve studied Greg as he left. His contentious bearing had been upstaged by the new guy. Either jealousy or admiration, Steve wasn't sure. Maybe if he scored something good tonight, it'd get his head straight.

37

Time was running out. There were only a few weeks until the storage space was no longer an option for band practice. The sound was improving, so they psyched themselves to play a real venue, live in front of an audience. They were still rough around the edges, mostly due to Steve's chronic lateness, but the majority agreed that a trial by fire performance was needed. Laney put on a brave face but had butterflies in her stomach. Ian talked her off the ledge.

"Don't expect to hit it out of the ballpark the first time. Set your sights too high, and you'll dispirit yourself. Nobody's first live gig is perfect."

Mitch busied himself by contacting various clubs. He learned that an opening act cancelled so a spot was available Sunday at Pop's Palace.

Steve had been told that the show started an hour earlier, so all the band would arrive at the same time.

Being a last-minute replacement didn't allow them time for a proper sound check. Ian suggested they open their set with a different song, out of necessity. This song would roll out each member's contribution separately. Rhythm guitar, lead guitar, drums, a bass drop then Greg's vocals. It was a gutsy move, so the sound man could mix the band before the audience caught on.

Sure enough, it worked. Now that the set list had alternated, Ian and Laney took turns calling out the next numbers, to varying degrees of success.

Laney surprised herself at how natural some of the songs poured out of her. Other songs were a struggle. She had a hard time making eye contact with the audience. One look of disapproval would throw off her game.

Paul appeared to be having stagefright, but soldiered on, hitting all marks with his Telecaster.

Steve did whatever Steve wanted, including amusing himself by flinging a drumstick or two at Greg for fun. Greg ignored them to the best of his ability, slinking about without missing a note. He knew how to engage the crowd in his own fashion. As usual, Ian did his best to corral them when things veered off course.

At the end of the set, the audience's clapping ended too short. Hardly the response Laney had hoped.

The band went to the backstage, passing the next act, Baragon's Rainbow. That band's appearance had the hippy template down pat.

Once they were out of sight, Greg put Steve in a chokehold. "Fucker! What's the deal with the drumsticks?"

Steve broke free and parried with a punch to the ribs. The brawl was on, the two grappling and shoving and getting in some solid hits. In the blink of an eye, it was over when both were restrained by the rest of the band and a circle of others. In the melee, Laney took a stray elbow near her left eye which knocked her behind some equipment. Everybody turned their attention to her.

"Guys, guys, I'm okay! Settle down, settle down, shit!"

Once the two were led to separate areas, only the muffled music of Baragon's Rainbow could be heard.

Ian had seen this before and was ready to close the chapter on this band. He'd foolishly allowed himself to get his hopes up, for a fresh face like Laney's. Foolish to think that this time would be different.

One of Pop's Palace's employees was a med student who pressed a cold, damp rag on Laney's forehead, which had grown a bruise near her eye. He thought it would be fine, but told her to get it looked at it by a doctor, to be on the safe side.

38

The next morning, her eye had swollen shut, and was leaking. She couldn't decide what was worse: the pain, or her stupidity in not taking care of her eye immediately. It hadn't looked that bad when she got home. She made it to the local walk-in clinic and waited. And waited. All the insipid chatter and scuffing, and crying babies in the waiting room compounded her misery. Finally her name was called. A short, blonde heavy-set nurse with square bifocals delicately washed around the damaged area, applied ointment to her eye then added a cold compress to it.

"That looks nasty. What's your level of pain, one being none, to ten being worst?"

"I'd say, six, no, seven. Aaaand, emotionally, a ten."

"I have to ask you a series of questions. How did this happen?"

"I was playing in a rock band last night, then a fight broke out."

"Is there more you'd like to share?"

"Pretty much it. All I remember, anyway."

"Young lady, this is a safe environment. You can tell me anything you want."

"Look, I may be . . . addled at the moment, but are you talking about what I think you're talking about?"

"Do you have a significant other?"

"Not anymore."

"Since when? Did this person do this to you?"

"Whaaa? No! That's crazy."

"Please understand that whatever you say stays between you and me. You didn't do anything wrong and you need to break contact with this person."

"It's not what you think." Laney sighed.

"Young lady, I must say, your story is a new one on me. I've met countless 'clumsy' women, who return time and again."

The push-me-pull-you conversation continued in this vein for over two hours, which may not have lasted as long had Laney kept her indignity in check.

Finally, Laney was released with a week's worth of ointment and gauze in one hand, a women's shelter business card in the other. She almost tossed it, but changed her mind. What was the name of that girl from high school? Carly? The one who got married after graduation? Whose marriage quickly became a one-sided boxing match and those same excuses made the rounds. Between today's interrogation and yesteryear's guilt, she was emotionally well past eleven.

39

Things were falling into place in Turnbul. The money coming in helped Arthur not sweat the small stuff as much as before. His underworld cronies only knew the no-nonsense side of him. The reinvented and refined Arthur entranced those who attended his charity galas. Said attendees had borrowed jewelry, designer dresses, and most importantly, deep pockets. They were as delighted as children playing dress up, getting photo ops, more concerned about raising awareness to their brand than they were about Turnbul. He picked up quickly how easily egos could be massaged. This ambitious stratagem exceeded all expectations. If the deadline for Turnbul was delayed for a time, all the better. He was fine-tuning his words for public consumption, whether it was as a television guest or host to town hall meetings. He'd been ruminating over the histrionics of his first speech. It could grow tiresome quickly. He could admonish detractors in a low-keyed voice just as easily.

This philanthropist angle was almost too easy. To the point, when he was staring at the darkness late at night, it almost felt he didn't deserve it somehow. They may have been thoughts drudged up by the phone discussion with Bishop Alexie. Arthur's solution was never to seek absolution, but to bury himself in more work. It was now time to turn his attention to Tungsten Heights.

40

Steve had checked out for a time, doing God knows what. Ian and Mitch spent a lot of time talking. Paul was filling out job applications. Greg stayed inside for the rest of the week, watching TV while getting stoned until his lady, Violet, came home from work. She was a fetching brunette, tall and rail-thin who let Greg do most of the speaking. Something in her past made her look beyond his obvious foibles. She adored him, and he let her adore him. She'd never seen him perform on stage since he moved to Pittsburgh. He'd convinced her that he'd be unable to concentrate. He volunteered little of his past, but he was funny and sexy and she was content to come home to him.

Laney was disappointed but not deterred. She looked in the mirror at her discolored eye. It was healing and so was she, spiritually. She had actually played live with a band, something she'd never dared back in Maryland. Here she was, by herself, invested in this new life. She had no choice but to double down on this wild-ass flight of fancy.

•　　•　　•

Ian, in a fit of surrender, humored Mitch's idea to keep the band together. A flurry of texts later, they finally all agreed to meet mid-week.

The next morning, 10:38 AM, Ian and Mitch picked up Laney in a leased 2013 Subaru Impreza for brunch. Since Ian had quit his job, he'd had to downgrade. The lease was due to expire anyway. They decided to hash things out at an old diner. Not a nouveau diner resembling a quaint throwback, but a real greasy spoon. Its dingy character, built up decades ago, had somehow lasted long enough for tastes to change back to romanticism about simpler times. Upon entering, Laney couldn't help but notice the solemn near-silence of the customers, the waiters, everybody.

"So . . . did someone die?"

Ian shushed her off with a finger over his lips, all the while grateful that Laney's voice had been too low for others to hear.

"Steelers lost big last night," Ian said in a sharp whisper. He was trying to yell and be quiet at the same time. "We take football very seriously here. The day after a loss is a day of mourning. You should start paying attention to more football if you really want to fit in here."

41

The day of reckoning came. The band was again assembled at Ian's place. Greg showed up early. Weeks of unclogging the drain with Violet had mellowed him considerably. Steve showed up to receive a big hug from Greg. Greg didn't even goof on Steve's bad breath. Steve looked like he was tired of the fighting. It had taken a toll on him. He was smiling. Maybe he'd resolved some personal issues. Paul finally showed up, leaner and wearing his latest headgear, a chapeau, which Greg immediately yanked off.

"Dude, everyone knows you're balding. You're bald! You are bald! Own it! Now that you dropped a few, get some t-shirts with obscure bands from the past. And the Van Dyke is workin' for you, I shit you not. All that's left is a clean shave on the melon and you've got it! Think I don't want my band to look its best?"

Paul grinned. He'd never been told he'd be cool. Not even by his ex-wife.

Now that the negativity, for now, was swept aside. Mitch related all the bullet points laid out by Laney and Ian. Among the words of wisdom: Don't suck as much. The gig after that, suck less, and keep working until you stop sucking. Then comes the bucket of money.

• • •

Relieved of their taskmaster duties, Laney and Ian sat on the couch, bouncing ideas about the band's direction. Songwriting was truncated and saved for future conversations. Laney had spotted a stack of *Freeloader* newspapers. Sharpsburg didn't carry them and she wanted to catch up. Ian said he wasn't done reading them and he'd give them to her when he'd finished. She rattled through them as a kid would a gift on Christmas day. She opened up the music section. Ian rubbed his eyes.

She studied the music review section page as one would the Dead Sea scrolls.

TUNESBURY
By Carl Drummond
The Demands, Baragon's Rainbow, Snivelers Inc.
Pop's Palace Sunday night.

Opening act, The Demands, did anything but demand attention, unless you like circus acts. The set started with a modicum of expected professionalism, if little sparkle. Songwriter/rhythm guitarist and occasional vocalist Laney Kilburn can't seem to decide if she's Jessica Lea Mayfield or The Cocktail Slippers. Some songs were catchy, with colorful lyrics and others were more suited for fist-pumping rock anthems done to death in the '80s. Lead singer, Greg Burdette, had the frontman archetype down pat. Credit to him for selling pedestrian songs. The rest of the band put on a perfunctory show that degenerated during the last few songs. The lead guitarist should have been arrested for loitering. It's as if the group formed earlier that day at a guitar store. The sole musician who stood out was songwriter/bassist Ian Hurst, who's knowledgeable playing kept this motley band grounded.

More so than the drummer, who could greatly benefit by using a metronome. You could tell which
songs were more Kilburn and which were more
Hurst. The mash-up of styles caused confusion at
times. Kilburn only stood out as the token female
in the band. Cute in a wounded-bird sort of way.
Her nervousness was charming at times. All this
effort wasted on tepid material.

The article continued coverage of Baragon's Rainbow
and Snivelers Inc.'s performances but Laney couldn't care
less. She rolled up the paper, stood, and stomped in Mitch's
direction. She wanted to mangle the paper and have a good
cry, but not in front of the band. Her only outlet now was
rage. Knowing the pointlessness of yelling at non-responsive
newsprint, Mitch became the target. She swatted the back of
his head with the paper.

"You there! I *knew* we weren't ready to perform live! *Why
didn't we wait, Mitch? Why did you do this to me? To us!"*

Steve rolled his eyes before went to the bathroom to take a
piss. Greg casually preened about, lighting his cigarette. Ian's
home had been smoke free until now, but what did it matter?

"People have short memories, Laney. Each performance
will be better than the last one, and staying holed up, practicing doesn't prepare you to play before paying customers. Plus,
our collective funds are drying up, so we have to put ourselves
out there now if we want to eat later."

Greg leaned against a window sill, away from the band.

"For a guy who didn't like us, he sure seems sweet on you,
Laney. Maybe you could, y'know, take one for the team."

"How 'bout *you* taking one for the team, Greg!" said Laney.

Greg's face betrayed a rare moment of bewilderment. He
swaggered out, not as smoothly as usual. The other bandmates

did their best to stifle laughter, some unable to hold it until he was out of earshot.

"Oh dear, I believe you've ruffled his plumage," Ian said.

42

The next day, Laney woke with a clearer head. She'd allowed herself to get too worked up last night but the sun would still shine. At least she hoped it was shining, not having windows to peer out.

She met Mitch in Oakland to discuss the band's future, get some coffee and window shop. They left a used book store with two plastic bags each.

"Surely there's a term for when the blood drains from your fingers when you carry these bags," Mitch said.

"Got it! Digiplasmitis! I just made it up. Oooh! That consignment shop just gave me a brainstorm! You know what you need, Mitch? A coooooool blazer."

"I have plenty of suit jackets from my old job."

"Not a suit jacket, just a little something that shows that you're a professional while maintaining your rock cred. You can wear it with a cool t-shirt underneath."

The clothes that adorned the shop were surprisingly affordable. Mitch eyed a glitzy red tuxedo jacket.

"Don't go with that. Too busy. And corny. A solid color, maybe a Khaki blazer would work better. You can still wear jeans to maintain your rocker status."

After rummaging through the store, Laney found two such

blazers and Mitch tried them on. Mitch had hated trying on clothes since he was a child. Mom would make him wear one piece of apparel after another while Mitch sulked. But for Laney, he'd give it a shot.

"That doesn't look good, it looks *great!* This one has a nice cut made for your frame. The other, not so much."

"Okay, Laney, now it's your turn. How about some dresses?"

"I dunno. Where would I go that I need a dress?"

"On stage. I get the whole Grunge look you've been going for, but—"

"It is so not a grunge look. These are all I have," she said, staring down at her worn jeans, ripped at the knees, and flip-flops.

"I think a dress will add a little sex appeal."

"Oh, you think I should just be eye-candy?"

"Don't get your back up. Open your mind to it. You're pretty and petite. I'm not asking you to dress like a prostitute. We're here anyway, why not? You roped me into trying on the blazer. Besides, you don't want Greg to have a monopoly on bringing the sexy."

That was all Laney needed to hear.

Laney tried on several dresses, to varying degrees of success. She was looking for nothing too glamorous or short. It'd be hard to focus on playing guitar without horny guys looking up her skirt. It was mutually agreed that two dresses and one blazer would be the purchase. Mitch took everything to the counter to pay, but Laney wanted to buy her own clothes. Besides, they were only twenty dollars apiece.

"That's a fine blazer you picked out, sir," said the cordial old cashier who was probably the store owner. "It was owned by Mister Clarke, the snappiest dresser I knew. Never left the house unkempt."

"Guess I just got lucky. Why would he get rid of this?"

"Oh, his widow got rid of his clothes. It reminded her too much of him. Poor Debbie."

"Mitch, if you want, we can look elsewhere."

"Nah. It's almost like fate found this for me. Hah. Listen to me, all New Age and shit."

"Well, young man, just take good care of that. Wouldn't want to disgrace Mister Clarke's memory."

Mitch probably already did that the moment he wore it.

43

Ian's old flame, Charlotte, offered her garage for The Demands' practice space. Ian had mixed emotions. He and Charlotte had parted as friends but being around her more often might muddy the waters. Nonetheless, he accepted her generosity.

Licking their wounds, The Demands pressed on, not letting something as miniscule as a bad review deter them. That fucker who wrote it would be the same fucker begging for an interview next year. Never underestimate the power of spite. As a unit, they were cramming for the finals. Sure enough, more sessions and free live shows educated them on what worked and what didn't. The flubs were becoming fewer. Mitch wasn't choosey about the locale. They performed for four people at a bistro with the same furor as they would hopefully play one day in packed nightclubs. Store openings, Mexican restaurants, carnivals and more. They played a few benefit shows, including one for the Peters Foundation. That gig got the band's name mentioned in the standard papers that parents read. No bio or group photo, but the mention was enough. The point was getting exposure and dealing with the highs and lows. Cover songs now peppered the set list. Ian explained that it would help pique the audience's interest. She wasn't happy about it, but Laney accepted it as a means to an end.

Eventually, Mitch made arrangements to get the band a portion of the door. Not a lot, but it was baby steps. To Mitch and Ian, who had been paying the band out of their own pockets, it was validation.

More of the familiar faces showed up and some even knew the words to the songs. The band members' competitiveness forged a new sound uniquely theirs. And the sound was good. No one wanted to be the weak link. Whereas Steve kept his excesses offstage, Greg openly took every drink or drug offered to him, and somehow kept it together. When he mixed the wrong cocktail, he still maintained enough stamina to get the words right and improvised gesticulations entertainingly. One thing was certain, Greg was comfortable in his own skin. A snake skin, granted, but one that kept crowds in his thrall. This flew in the face of everything Ian believed in, but after all his experiences, this odd grouping might have the right elements to break big. Provided Greg lived long enough.

The Demands by now had played several haunts owned by Arthur Peters. Once, half-drunk, Arthur came on strong with plaudits that The Demands took as condescending and disingenuous. He'd repeatedly asked them to do some nice songs that weren't so noisy. The band considered him a slobbering, rich loudmouth who'd probably run them out of his gated community with guard towers and attack dogs.

•　　　•　　　•

Mitch was good at working a room, small talking with denizens of whatever watering hole they played. The longer they stayed, the more beer was sold and owners like Arthur Peters liked that at his bars. More than once, Mitch stood outside, handing out free pitchers of beer to passersby. All they had to do in return was to catch this hot local band. Mitch had to open up a new credit card account to handle such expenses. He was getting himself more in debt, but never let on.

One of Mitch's many duties included cheerleading the band even on those bad nights.

"I told you, no one bats a thousand, not even the biggest acts! It's just a matter of making the bad nights fewer and fewer until it comes natural as breathing. You're getting there, you're loosening up. I love the progress you're making, and you can even let it looser. Think showmanship!"

In the following weeks, they did just that, and to everyone's surprise, it was working. Now they were improvising stage theatrics. One night Laney showed up with a green short bob hairstyle with bangs. That would get them talking. Camera phones flashed and downloaded her new look. Half the people on social media responded favorably to her new 'do, the other half thought she'd forgotten the fans that got her where she was. Not that she was really anywhere yet. Five songs in, she revealed it was a wig and tossed it into the audience. Then she let her real hair down. There were shrieks of joy and laughter in the crowd and internet fans were united, at least for three minutes. Then the Monday morning quarterbacking commenced:

She should have waited until the show ended.
No, Asshat, that would have been too predictable.
I thought it was bangin'! Literally. Lol.
Just a retarded attention whore.
It got YOUR attention, didn't it, douche?
Fuck you.
That's what your mom said to me last night
That joke's so old, it's grown mold on it.
Really classy, dudes.

And so on . . .

Seeing The Demands wasn't a concert, it was now an experience.

44

Their fanbase was growing as their act did. Polished without looking polished. Paul was still without polish, period. He could kill some nights, but he couldn't keep it up night after night. He'd phone in his performances half the time, so the other members worked around him. The older acts had bass players stand stock still, like John Entwistle or Bill Wyman, so Ian did a role-reversal and found himself pulling the craziest stunts. Once his bass strap popped off and he leaned against the side of a speaker, shimmying his back down to the floor without missing a note. This one-off accident got uproarious cheers. He'd waited a decade for moments like this. But trying that a second time would be unlikely, so he'd come up with something else. Greg already had his part down. Steve insisted on bringing back the drum solo, so the others made a bit out of it, all turning around, staring at him, scratching their chins, pointing and mock-discussing his technique. The crowd ate that up as well. Best of all, the theatrics didn't cause the music to suffer. In fact there were happy accidents that they'd file away for future gigs and songs. Even music reviewer Carl Drummond had changed his tune about The Demands.

The band needed to keep the ball moving before fans found a new band to latch onto. Mitch insisted Laney journal on

Twitter and other social media, which cost her sleep. Mitch's number one rule for her was "Ignore the online haters." Other bandmates contributed, but it was evident that Laney and Greg had the most followers, for the horny men and women. Laney also had the support of the online girl-power community who helped her through some rough days. The growing fanbase not only rooted for them, but some had joined them as unpaid roadies. Roadies who could help loading and unloading equipment. One of them had a moving truck he'd bought for pennies on the dollar at a police auction of impounded cars. Perfect for storing the drums and speakers. The band led by example with the setting up. All except Greg, who considered menial chores beneath him. Sometimes Steve would pitch in, sometimes he did his disappearing act until show time.

A few months in, The Demands began to headline larger clubs. They also got billed on a three-day outdoor music festival to benefit an autism treatment center. The festival had dozens of local acts that covered the spectrum: Rockablilly, hip-hop, metal, ska, world music, funk, emo, etcetera. The festival would end late Sunday with the sole national act, Three Quarters and a Nelson. TQ&N had an edgy Metallica sound. They'd gotten their start in the 'Burgh and were greeted as returning heroes.

The Demands were scheduled mid-day on Saturday, which wasn't ideal, given the heat, but the festival would be great exposure.

•   •   •

Greg had gone full-court diva, delaying the time-slot considerably until the following act had to take their place. The promoter threatened to toss the band out. The other Demands members knew Greg had fostered his own fanbase, so going on without him would be an embarrassment.

"What's with you, man?" Mitch said to Greg's unresponsive face.

Finally, at dusk, The Demands were told to play or leave. Laney now had a headache and the rest of the band built up a head of steam, shooting hard glances Greg's way. Time was shrinking and Greg's too-cool-for-the-room demeanor wasn't cute anymore. A frazzled Mitch took a hit from a roadie's blunt.

"Time's up! Get your asses up there or leave, now!" shouted the promoter.

"Why, yes sir, sir," Greg said as he lifted himself out of the beach chair. "Well, what are you clowns starin' at? Let's do it to it."

The Demands' staring contests had become routine now.

"What the fuck just happened?" said Paul, incredulously.

They took to the stage, to peals of screams. The band waved hello out to the biggest grouping of heads and arms they'd ever seen from a stage.

The setting sun behind The Demands served as supernatural Klieg lights. The small red marble set in purple clouds created a sensational, dramatic effect.

Greg had played it just right to get the best Saturday time slot.

That brilliant, brilliant bastard, Ian thought.

The Demands upgraded from great exposure to fantastic exposure. Greg could act like a chooch, but he was also very canny when it served his purpose.

•　　•　　•

The Demands crushed it. Neither they, nor the crowd, wanted their set to end, but other acts needed their day in the sun, so to speak.

Backstage, Greg was now the hero. Beer cans snapped open. Laney's beer spurted out a geyser of foam directly into her face and soaked her hair.

"Ooh! Yeeeeeah-ha-ha, mothaaaa-fuckas! We did it!" Laney said, raising her beer in celebration. Everyone clapped. The day was made.

That night, The Demands felt that, yes, they could go national someday. Mitch had disappeared for a time, but returned with a present; the members of Three Quarters and a Nelson, the show-closers for Sunday night. The Demands shot out of their various positions and sputtered reverential words like Gatling guns. They even hung with these seasoned musicians at their party tent. Both bands got on surprisingly well. Paul came out of his shell, happy to meet names he'd respected for years. Laney and Ian talked music and technique with this time-tested band. Greg and Steve gravitated to the heavy partiers, learning nothing but new ways to get fucked up and raise hell. Mitch picked brains at times, extracting the formula for staying power. But not overmuch. This was The Demands' time. Maybe TQ&N could consider them as an opening act on tour? More cases of cold beer and more food continued to show up, one of the contract riders. Mitch opened a beer and fantasized about riders.

45

One glorious night does not a star make. The band was still near broke. They had a stream of new offers coming their way, but offers would take time, and the ones that passed the smell test would take even longer. Mitch had every flat surface covered in paperwork. One stack for recording contracts, another for club dates, another for promotional plans. He could have just done it all on the computer, but he could better assess his priorities if he saw them all physically. Screw the environment, he had a band to promote every waking moment.

After a few weeks of not seeing any money, save for meager living expenses, a pall had once again set in. The only thing good about becoming a local celebrity with no money was the free meals and beer offered by fans. Greg, in particular, took advantage of the situation, asking for free things and usually getting them. He was full of himself and started falling into his old habits, the worst being late for rehearsals. Steve was showing up on time, but his motive was always asking for money and he scowled when he didn't get it. But he asked every time, using another ploy. A sick relative, a friend's car repairs. He offered to sell them things, as long as they wouldn't worry about a receipt. Laney and Ian began feeling more flustered. But Mitch would smooth things over.

Just as the band were calling it a night, Laney chimed in as she stood and massaged her stiff back.

"You know what I'd like? A keyboardist. To add color."

The other band members were tired and couldn't contain their groaning.

"We're never going to make money. Next you'll want a horn section." Steve huffed and scratched his head repeatedly.

Ian and Mitch eyed each other. After all the time spent forming a decent band, Laney now wanted a keyboardist. Mitch may have been manager, but he considered himself more of a facilitator of Laney and Ian's wishes. Time to make another miracle.

Mitch knew well of Ian's experience as utility player for other bands in the Pittsburgh area and suggested Ian make the club rounds solo. The rest of the band took time off to unwind.

Ian met an old friend one night, Eddie Gorski. Eddie sported a full beard and his dark red hair was pulled back, samurai-style. He knew his shit and had a good rep. His previous band had broken up a month ago. One session with The Demands was all it took to make him a member.

46

One afternoon, Greg was running late again. His "I'll be there shortly" phone call was a slight improvement. Time was killed with gossip, jokes, and sharing new music ideas. More than two hours passed and the small talk was wearing thin.

"You're really rockin' your new black eye-liner look, Laney."

"You think it's too much, Mitch?"

"No, it looks hot."

A series of "oh, yeah's" came from from three fans-slash-roadies who were just hanging out.

Then Laney silently craned her neck towards the entrance. Greg casually walked in with a carafe of wine in one hand, a half-full glass in the other. Ian shook his head disapprovingly, not caring if it was noticed. Mitch met Greg half-way.

"Thank you, oh one of great voice. What a great refurbishing your presence has visited upon us today."

"Judge not lest ye be judged," Greg retorted casually before taking a sip of wine.

"You know, every time someone quotes that line, they think it's a get-out-of-jail-free card. I call bullshit. If you're serious about staying in this band, you need to show some dedication, if not just consideration for the others."

"I'm the one bringin' the results. I made that festival show blow us up big, and haven't seen dime one since."

"That festival booking wouldn't have happened if I didn't pull some strings!"

Greg's face dropped to a forlorn expression.

"I guess I'm the bad guy here," Greg said calmly.

"Don't turn this shit back on me! The charm you pull on the ladies doesn't fly with me."

"Well, let's hear you sing."

"That's not in my job description."

Blurting that out embarrassed him to no end, having heard that enough times from douchebags at Devinshire Concepts.

"Here I was, ready to bring it, and you go all Reuben Kincaid on me! I'm the one people come to see, which makes me the ring-leader. You got nothin' without me!" he said, jabbing his thumb on his chest. Greg tossed back the remaining contents of his glass.

"Fucking buzzkill is all you are! Enjoy your evening!" Greg walked out, but stopped at the sidewalk. He turned back to brandish his glass in Mitch's direction.

"Except you. Go find some paperwork to fill out. You need to improve if we're going to make money." Greg punctuated his statement by slamming his glass to the ground, which had its desired effect. The band, stunned into silence, clumsily fumbled with instruments and amps. The non-band members hastily found things to busy themselves with, including picking up the glass.

Ian was the rock that Laney could usually count on for support, and the feeling was mutual. Seeing her sink with resignation almost shut him down. Finally, her eyes met his. Without words, they told each other *We'll get through this*. It was becoming an increasingly common psychic form of reassurance between them.

•   •   •

Laney cleared her throat, then swigged from her water bottle.

"Guys. I've been meaning to try out this new song, if you're up to it."

There was no objection.

"It's mid-tempo, starts in A minor for the first 8 measures, then I repeat the first 8 measures, but this time Ian and Steve join in with bass and light drumming to add tension. Eddie, you come in on the main melody line in the key of C. You won't know it until you hear me switch to it, so just listen during this dry run. You'll catch this on the second pass. This song's only half-written so this is me working out the rest as it comes. Any input is cool with me. I have to get this down now."

This was her safe place. The many songs she'd written in her Maryland bedroom were crap, more emotional releases than anything. Lately, her songs covered dark subjects and emotions, with an increased incorporation of minor chords. The kind of songs you'd listen to at night when you would question choices in life, or a bad relationship. Certainly not Emo music, but a side of her that blossomed lately. She'd written enough straight-up rockers that these more personal songs balanced out the set list nicely.

47

Arthur continued his public presence, pressing flesh with more businessmen with companies that could use increased visibility in a down market. Arthur wasn't above shaming those who asked too many questions. This was the internet era, after all. *Remember your company that had the industrial accident, killing nine people in 1998?* Arthur would make a point to remind the populace that the anniversary of that act was fast approaching. If it bleeds it leads, as they say in the press. If it's a slow news day, anniversaries of tragedies always helped fill airtime. Even those who grudgingly complied with his requests, spun these shakedowns into promotional altruism for the cameras. The reutilization plan for Tungsten Heights was shaping up nicely. A hefty chunk of change that surely would please Arthur's higher-ups. He was aglow.

48

Laney was at her apartment, changing to warm and dry socks. She put on a pot of tea to warm herself up. The heat from the stove began to revive her. She locked her gaze into the stove iron, as it glowed red. The watched pot never boils, but right now, Laney couldn't give a damn. No songs came to her, and she was forcing herself to make it happen. Her living conditions sucked, the band was not getting along, and she almost believed the triumphant night at the festival was a fever dream. If you work hard enough and knew why you were put on this messed up planet, things should be improving, right? A lot of it was in the timing. All the pieces seemed to be in place, but what the fuck did she know about forming a rock band? She held a secret resentment towards her neediness of Ian to make her songs work. Her grandiose plan to front a band that followed her blindly was met by the sobering reality that she didn't have all the tools to make it happen. Ian was cool and all, but this wasn't what she envisioned. Why wasn't a new song coming to her? Too many emotions flooding, with no musical outlet. She shamefully dreamt that the print shop would take her back. Most of her songs were inspired by her mood swings, but why bother when you felt universally ignored? Hours later, several cups of tea in her, Laney's focus turned to the grain in the hardwood floor, and nothing else.

"Rrrrrrrgh . . ." she railed through gritted teeth. She wanted to scream at the ceiling, to vent, kick shit around, but Margo was asleep hours ago, most likely. Although Margo wasn't the most pleasant person, Laney treated her the way she would hope to be treated when she was withered and feeble.

Maybe it was the universe's way of telling her tonight was about decompressing. Too bad she arrived at this thought in the wee hours. She was so steadfast in her rock star plans, she wasn't in the present to enjoy the journey. She was becoming a workaholic at age twenty-two when most people are socializing and enjoying themselves. Laney feared that from now on, she'd forever have tunnel vision, discarding all pleasure to push herself even harder. If success came, would she recognize the person in the mirror?

She missed her grandfather, who she hadn't seen in years. He'd handed down his vinyl records and old turntable. Neither would fit in the car when she moved away. She found the songs online, but the full experience of listening through crackles always inspired her. Also, that Muddy Waters bootleg was impossible to replace. Rock 'n' roll was the one connection they'd made and he'd answered all her questions. He spoke of seeing Led Zeppelin, Pink Floyd, and other top acts in stadiums. Whatever happened to rock stars anyway? She wanted so hard to be one, the kind of musical act that thousands of people would pay top dollar to see. Not to mention people who would pay more for scalped tickets.

Winning over the curs who populated The Hotseat would be the toughest hurdle. She once again subjected herself to watching more humiliation of acts in mid-performance. It got her pilot light relit. It didn't matter that The Hotseat wasn't a legitimate part of the Pittsburgh music scene. She was going to win those drunken bastards over and they wouldn't know what hit them.

The worst of the winter was over. But Pittsburgh wouldn't let go of the fierce cold for months. Wind and slush everywhere kept people miserable. The garage door was closed and the band was surrounded by donated space heaters. Ian was uncharacteristically absent until he knocked on the garage door. Once he was let in, it was obvious there was a renewed spirit in his stride. The rest of the band were nonplussed.

"Lady . . . and gentlemen, come out with me."

He led the others around the corner, where they saw an abnormally large van.

"Here's our tour bus. It's actually a vanpool bus. Seats fifteen people. The idea clicked when a friend told me his commuter van was switched for a newer model. It wasn't hard to hunt down the company that supplies these for the government's vanpool program. Surprisingly affordable, probably because there's no AC or heat. Once we rip out all the seats, we can fit most of our gear in here."

"This is so many greats!" Laney said.

Ian took the band out for a long ride and they left the infighting behind. They were fired up, goofing around, doing donuts and even broke out into song. By night's end, everyone tapped out and parted ways.

49

Laney took the last bus route home. She was coming down from the high of the joyride. It had been a long day. She found herself now feeling lonely and very tired.

Her stop was the last on the line. The driver told her to watch out for ice as she stepped off. She gave a hushed thanks to the driver. Once her feet hit the slush and pavement, the ear-splitting pop and hiss of the bus's air brakes jostled her alert. Bothersome as it was, the noise kept her on her feet and she found they could commence walking. The soft guitar case slung on her back was an oppressive weight tonight. Only a few blocks scuffling with wet socks and wind-bruised cheeks and she could ooze into bed.

"'Ey, there."

Laney's eyes were half-closed and she never looked to see who spoke.

"Sorry, I'm strapped for cash."

Laney gradually increased the speed of her walk, doing her best not to be obvious.

"Come back, honey!"

That was a different voice. There were now two men behind her.

She broke into a hard sprint to the best of her ability. She was a good runner, but the combination of exhaustion, confusion, and slippery footing made her clumsy.

Her dash was cut short by a slick spot on the sidewalk.

Her knee gave out when it hit the ground. She could hear the strange men breathing. Then she felt weightless. She was being lifted like a ragdoll, the straps of her guitar case violently wrested off non-working arms. Then she fell again, hurting all over. She heard a zipping noise and feared the worst. The sound was her guitar case being yanked open. The same guitar that had shared all those miles with her.

One of the men grunted while opening the contents.

Through a herculean effort, Laney managed to lurch her body over so she could see her assailants. But the lighting was bad. When the grunter did his best to examine the guitar, the only thing that showed clearly were the deep scratches Laney had gouged on it. At his angle, it was illegible and just looked like a damaged old guitar.

Angered, he hurled it down the curb, where it burst open a discarded trash bag. The bad lighting worked in her favor, so she'd keep the guitar.

"Ahhh! Can't get shit for this. Look, it's all scraped! But we're gonna get something out of this, one way or another . . ." Laney finally saw a smallish silhouette perch behind Mr. Grunt. By the shape, it was most likely the other man who'd chased her.

"Dude! Shit, petty theft is a slap on the wrist. What you're lookin' at is prison time! Besides, I'm freezin' my ass off. Let's go!"

The large man looked around and heard sirens approaching from blocks away. Most likely a fire truck, but the bright lights could also be police. Either way, these two weren't accustomed to doing their thing in the glare of lights. The two ran away, slapping slush in their wake.

Her spur-of-the-moment scraped Demands logo had saved her guitar. And very likely saved her from a sexual assault. Her tormenters long gone, Laney fished her filthy guitar from the garbage, held it tight as she could and shivered on the street as she sobbed. For how long, she didn't know.

50

Arthur's mental gymnastics worked overtime, cobbling up the usual suspects to carry out his instructions to the letter for Tungsten Heights. When not making headline generating appearances, he spent a lot of time with the organization's number crunchers. Painstakingly detailing the arithmetic for the mob's slush fund, based on mercurial speculations. At times, it took a physical toll on Arthur, so he promised his wife he would lose weight. Once he began cutting down his eating portions, he felt better for a time. But that, too, was work. At times, the old Arthur would resurface, and his impatience occasionally flared like his hemorrhoids. Lightning rarely struck twice, so Arthur was determined not to be a one-hit wonder. By hook or by crooks, Tungsten Heights would be his. Brought to him by the corporation of good intentions.

51

Laney called in sick, saying she had the flu and needed some time to rest. Mitch bought it. She'd been stretching herself thin lately, he thought. When the rest of the band showed up, they worked out other parts of songs until she'd get better. A few days stretched to a week. She must have gotten the bug bad. Finally, Mitch checked up on her. She needed a few more days.

The few more days became another full week. When Laney showed up early for band practice, Ian and Mitch let her know how great it was to have her back in the saddle. When they went for a hug, Laney begged off.

"I might still be contagious, dudes."

Mitch and Ian took her at her word, then caught her up on the headway Ian and the others had made in her absence. She half-smiled but remained low-key.

Twenty minutes passed. Paul showed up, but the wannabe glimmer twins were the only hold ups. Mitch paced around the garage, updating the promotional schedule for the next month.

Laney sat cross-legged on the floor, studiously adjusting the strings on her guitar's headstock.

"Laney?" said Ian.

Laney, not looking up, continued her prep. "Mmm?"

"I have to get this out or I'll go batshit," Ian said in a low voice as he kneeled down.

"I'm more than a bit . . . concerned, okay, worried about Steve. Bad enough Greg is a one-man opium den, but he somehow keeps it together. Steve may end up at the point of no return. When Mitch calls him, Steve drones incoherently, or forgets conversations entirely."

Laney, head still down, replied in a monotone, "Dude's not always the best at time-keeping, but you gotta admit, his fills add flavor. Once it impairs his abilities, we'll look into it."

Ian, taken aback by Laney's coldness, did a double take, stood up and walked away, his mind awhirl.

Just then, Steve showed up, with a harsh cough.

"Don't tell me you got the bug thing, too," Laney lied.

"K-huh. Somethin', like goin' 'round n'at, I guess."

"By my duffle bag, there's some cough syrup if you need it." Cough syrup being Laney's prop to explain being MIA.

He took a swig before wiping his mouth with his wrist. Laney worked her guitar again, lost in her private universe.

Greg was the last to enter, ever the star.

"Let's get this show on the road!" Greg said, raising his arms like a carnival barker. So they did. Laney loosened up by the fourth song. It was much needed therapy.

52

Mitch made his semi-weekly call to his parents and braced himself for the usual disapproval guised as concern. They were still berating him about quitting his job. Surprisingly, this latest conversation wasn't as harsh as the last, so Mitch managed to contain his defensiveness.

Exhaling his relief, Mitch resumed his work on his laptop. Making deals to help expand the band's exposure. At Devinshire, he'd tired of the term 'branding' but here he was, doing exactly that. Only this time, it wasn't to market flanges, laser-surgery, or organic eggs. It was tapping into something he was passionate about. These long hours were far more satisfying and he was adept at multitasking. Also, he felt a part of something big and glorious that was about to break big. Multi-basking, essentially. He became a quick study of a business model he hadn't used professionally: bartering. If The Demands played an instrumental opening song for a podcast, the host's sound man would help them record their own songs with better production values. Hours passed and Mitch was ready to call it a night. He'd accomplished much tonight. Then his phone rang.

"Christ almighty, who's calling this late?"

"Mitch?"

"Yes, I'm Mi— Hey! Is this Dwayne?"

Dwayne Simons and Mitch had become close friends at Devinshire Concepts. Even after Dwayne fell victim to the company's layoffs, they periodically kept in touch. Dwayne got back on his feet after taking classes to become an actuary for Perry Insurance.

"Saw your mother the other day and I hear you quit your job? What's gotten into you?"

"Dwayne, I'm gonna sell it to you straight: I've had it with the corporate bullshit."

"You sure that's the right move? These are hard times. Look, I wish I was making the money you were and—"

"Let me ask you something. At seven, did you dream of being an actuary? Huh?"

Mitch waited until the pregnant pause was in its third trimester before resuming.

"I thought so. Well one of us is going to make a living doing something creative, and it's not you!"

His proclamation was met with a hang up. Immediately, Mitch wanted to retract those words, a cheap shot at a good friend. But he felt attacked on all fronts. By his parents, by some of the band members, and his own creeping self-doubts. And now Dwayne? It was too much. His objective of falling asleep was a lost cause now.

Turning his laptop back on, Mitch finally noticed Ian standing zombie-like in the hallway, wearing only his boxer shorts and socks on his hands.

"Mitch . . . as soon as you can afford it, you gotta get your own place."

53

Mitch got his own place: A studio apartment with the first three months rent-free. 600 square feet, with a small inset kitchen that extended to the living room. Furniture would envelop it, so he did without for the most part. The bedroom was smaller than he'd like, but he only needed it for sleeping and/or fornicating. Best of all, his next door neighbor was out of town more often than not. Mitch was getting himself further in hock, with the addition of his new state-of-the-art computer. Instead of grabbing his old apartment's furniture from his parent's garage, he left the living room open for recording The Demands' first song, using his latest recording software. Mitch was running up a substantial bill on his credit cards. The band saw his setup and were agreeable. Laney was crestfallen, but did her best to hide it. This was hardly the Abbey Road experience she'd dreamt of, but it was a rush to hear music she made played back. Educational, too. If this was a way to get their music out quicker, she had to get with the times.

Mitch may have read the tutorials, but Ian took to the recording applications quicker. Ian showed the others some tricks on the software, and Laney began warming up to the idea.

Steve's drums wouldn't fit in Mitch's small apartment, so

Mitch bought a stripped-down electronic version to use in close quarters. This was a test, after all. Steve's drumming was just right, but Ian had to walk Paul through some of his parts. Paul was a follower, solid but lacking the limelight mindset of a lead guitarist. A handful of rough demos, some better than others, were recorded. It was a clunky, unfamiliar affair that improved with each take. Playing at a club was one thing, but a squeaky chair or sneeze during recording was harder to deal with. Ian was convinced he could learn how to edit out background noises. After the third time a car alarm blared, they covered the windows with makeshift curtains and other found objects. Steve and Greg raced out to grab sound-muffling items from a nearby dumpster. In a short time, the living room became a mess, between the dumpster juice, spilt beverages and Greg's cigarette butts. At least those two whack jobs were having fun and not bellyaching.

"This is why we can't have nice things," Mitch said.

It was a long day, and the band eventually got tired of playing the same songs.

"Can you add some echo chamber as that last song fades?" Ian suggested.

Mitch complied, and they liked what they heard.

"Who gives a shit about that? Just let me lay down my vocals so I can get on with my life." One thing you could never fault Greg for, he had no governor and always spoke his mind.

54

In Miami, Anatoly Nevelskoi was reading recent news on his phone. The way his granddaughter had taught him. As was his daily routine, he'd start by viewing photos of sexy starlets, then check the latest news, world events, the latest gadgets and baubles his wife might like, and the lottery results over his breakfast. Then it was down to business, checking on his empire. His nationwide satellite subordinates updated him on the latest tidings. One of his soldiers told him to check out the happenings in Pittsburgh. Pittsburgh had been a smooth operation, and Anatoly was eager to refresh his problem-solving acumen.

To Anatoly's shock, he saw a screenshot of Arthur Peters at a ribbon-cutting ceremony in Turnbul. Anatoly tossed his phone across the room, knocking over an expensive lamp.

"What in the *fuck* does Artur think he's doing?"

"Actually, his earnings have increased—" said an aide.

"Don't you ever open your mouth to me, you hear? He's going high profile! In case you haven't noticed, we don't have a PR department for a reason!"

Anatoly made contacts to the local talent, best equipped at cleaning up messes. Arthur's high visibility had put them in DEFCON 1 mode and needed a quick solution.

55

Keyboardist Eddie Gorski entered the room with an un-usually peppy spring in his step.

"Hey, man, you look chipper."

"More than chipper . . ." Eddie's neck muscles strained, accompanying a wide grin.

"Allie's pregnant! Isn't that awesome?"

The straight-faced mute responses suggested otherwise.

"We can't have this, Eddie," Laney said.

"Cah-mahn, Mitch! Tell me she's not serious!"

Laney stood up, one hand on her hip.

"Come watch us when you're not chasing babies some-day," Laney said stone-faced.

"Can't we—"

"No, Eddie. Break this barrier, and soon we'll have kids and spouses underfoot. This ain't a daycare center. I'm both happy and sad for you."

Now everybody was unnerved at Laney's comments. Mitch was assigned the role as manager, but the chain-of-command shifted to Laney in just a few sentences. Given Mitch's corpo-rate background, he would have made a similar statement, but one-on-one with Eddie, in a way that would soften the blow. Laney had now raised the stakes.

"Mitch! What do you say?"

A pause.

"I'm in agreement, and if anybody doesn't like Laney's decision . . . deal with it."

A dejected Eddie ambled his way out.

"Well, that was quick. Didn't have time to remember his last name, poor bastard," said Greg.

Ian knew Eddie all too well, and remained maudlin the rest of the day. This one last shot at glory was costing him money and relationships. Was it worth it?

56

More days, more practices. No time for a new keyboardist. They pushed onward.

"Laney, I was thinking, we could turn the solo of 'Hamstrung' into a double solo. I could play a descending scale while Paul plays an ascending scale. You can do bass. Think we could pull that off?"

"I think we should try it out tonight. What say you, Paul?"

"Sure. Right."

At this point, when Ian and Paul weren't playing together, they never spoke. Ian had tired of pushing the boulder that was Paul uphill and Paul was tired of Ian riding him. This did not go unnoticed by Laney.

"Look, Pauly. You either wanna grind out killer notes or stink up the place, but there's no room in this band for apathy!" she said.

"And here I thought feeling insulted was Paul's go-to emotion," Greg said.

Fuck off!" She caught a few breaths before resuming.

"I'll give it to you, you're proficient, but a hundred percent robot! You should be selling yourself to the crowd! If you don't commit, then you're a fucking roadblock." Laney never had such a filthy mouth before starting the band. Now her conversations were festooned with colorful curse words. Many a time, Laney had to be the intermediary, but this was the first time she'd laid into him. Paul just about had it. If The

Demands weren't getting so much heat from the music press, he'd bail out in a heartbeat. If it wouldn't work out, he could take his experience and name recognition to another band.

Finally, after a long absence and rumors of a break-up, The Demands resumed touring with a vengeance. Word of mouth and positive reviews built up over time. Of all the locales The Demands played, The Silverfish was their favorite and vice versa. Jerry DeSantis loved the band and gave them an open door policy. Any nights not booked, they worked out new material. It was one of the crappiest buildings they ever played, but the townies latched on to The Demands as *their* local band. It didn't matter that The Demands didn't live in Tungsten Heights. Both the band and the crowd built a special rapport. Maybe because it was the one bright spot in an otherwise depressed neighborhood.

Mitch used that open-door policy to his advantage, by announcing last-minute shows as happenings over social media. With expectations built, the band had to work harder than ever. This daunting never-ending task was his life now. His diet consisted mostly of black coffee and meal-replacing protein bars.

The Beatles had been turned down by many record labels, told "Guitar groups were out." Fifty years later, it seemed it may have finally come true. But not if Mitch and The Demands could effect a sea change. Dave Grohl could only carry the rock 'n' roll torch so long. If Mitch's professional background taught him anything, it was to learn from successful people, not the ones who failed with chips still on their shoulders.

One obstacle that needed addressing was Steve. It didn't

help that he was a no-show at times. Ian and Mitch would make last-minute calls to friends that knew their way around a kit. Sometimes Steve would appear last-minute, sometimes not. Then there were times he showed up after a replacement started the first set and he'd fume. Steve said he was burning out between the practicing and gigging. Mitch accentuated the positive and accepted it as an X-factor until Steve got his shit together. Maybe the pressure was getting to him. Greg, at least, showed up to every gig, and his last-minute appearances were clearly theatrical. He excelled at vamping between songs with outrageous stories every night. The band couldn't tell which stories were real and which were conjured from the ether. Laney's singing voice had grown more confident after all the hours she'd put in. She could charm an audience, but Greg had a way of seducing them. Ian, ever the team player, accepted his role as musical director armed with his bass. As part of the rhythm section, Ian would inform the replacement drummers how the next song would go.

One night, Ian brought a drummer from a band he'd played with years ago. Frank Dillon, a blond bodybuilder with sleeveless shirts to show his guns, had been out of the game when he chose to pursue a career in environmental assessment and raise a family. However, he'd seen The Demands play, so he knew some of the new songs already and didn't need much direction from Ian. He knew his stint was temporary, but he was glad to get out of the house for a change, away from the wife and kids. Laney and Ian did another hasty run-through with Paul about rearranging the songs sans keyboards. For once, Paul listened with no resistance.

57

The Silverfish's bouncer was a tall cup of mocha grande with a short stalk of dreads named Martin Hudson. He had forearms like Popeye and shoulders like a linebacker. His usual state of dress was pajama bottoms, sandals and concert t-shirts. Most often force was not necessary to escort unruly guests. Incidents were smoothed out through negotiation. Things only got physical when rowdy drunks grew beer balls, thinking they could take him down. It never ended well for them.

Every time the band played there, Laney would give Martin a big hug before the two caught up on how they'd been doing since the last gig. This time, Laney griped about Eddie and how they were going to try to work around newer songs she'd built around the keyboards.

"My Auhnt gave me piano lessons as a kid. Hated it. *Hated it.* After a few years, she had me playin' at church. Heh. That first time I was so nervous but the congregation encouraged me. Even when I hit a bad note. Once I learned some Ray Charles gospel, it got a lot better. Then she took me to a John Legend concert, and I got the bug. I dug deep wi' Stevie Wonder, Leon Russell, Elton John. Then Little Richard—that was the stuff."

"When's the last time you played?"

"Been a while. I used to play at jazz clubs and stuff sometimes."

"Hey, why don't you sit in with us tonight?"

"Ah, you know you're my girl, but I don't know if I'd fit in."

"What's to fit in? Eddie's playing was pedestrian. His stuff was strictly mood background and occasional transitions."

Laney's winsome smile locked onto Martin.

Martin dialed his phone.

"Johnny can cover for me. He owes me a favor."

Some minutes later, a deafening sound could be heard outside the Silverfish. A snarling, sputtering sound. It was a classic Harley-Davidson. The rider was covered head-to-toe with leathers and a variety of chains. He resembled Greg Allman, with his white hair, beard, ponytail and sunken eyes. His Iron Cross medallion completed the portrait. Johnny Aloysius "Trouble" Macintyre had arrived from West Virginia.

"Hey, Trouble!" Johnny earned that nickname many years ago, and a smart person wouldn't inquire how. Martin tapped Johnny's arm and felt resistance that was more than muscle.

"I was hopin' you were still in town! Dag, you wearin' a brace?"

"Sewn-in Kevlar. That way, I take a spill, I c'n shake it off."

"You come heavy?"

"You call me here to ask stupid questions?"

"If you got time, I need someone to spell me for a while. I'm sittin' in with the band."

"Well, shee-it. No one done to'd me you had any talent."

Martin and Johnny were an unlikely pair, but a casual friendship had been forged in a Cloverton pool hall.

Johnny knew this black dude was in the wrong bar and thought he'd have the sense to leave. Once he saw the other regulars pile on him, Johnny knew this guy wasn't ever coming up. Johnny tossed a few of them off Martin. They found themselves back-to-back against a horde of angry rednecks who accused Johnny of being a traitor. Johnny made it clear that he sure-as-shit didn't invite the stranger, but they was fixin' to kill him if he hadn't stepped in. Half the bar cleared out. The foolhardy ones stayed until, one by one, they ended up a variety of twisted statues that made whimpering sounds. Johnny made it clear that savin' Martin didn't make them friends for life and wanted nothing else to do with him.

By happenstance, Martin and Johnny found themselves together a second time. Needless to say, they were no longer welcome in that county either, due to outstanding arrest warrants. Johnny was good at kicking ass and Martin suggested the vocation of a bouncer. Johnny knew how to best use shadows for camouflage, so it suited him just fine. He'd stay in town for a while until he got into trouble, then he'd vanish, staying one step ahead of authorities.

58

Martin introduced himself to The Demands.

"Hello, gents! Laney said I could toss in on keyboards."

"Did she, huh?" said Ian.

"Got my bona fides n' everything. You are looking at a proud member in good standing of the Black Rock Coalition," Martin said while bowing as a sign of respect.

"So what are you, a coal miner?" Greg said.

"Vernon Reid? Living Colour? He was like, the founder. Nothing?"

"Yeah, 'Cult of Personality' . . . Always liked that song," Ian said.

"I got experience from playing clubs few years back in Oakmont. But the last place I played closed down and I was pullin' some serious cash. Kinda lost my heart for it, so I been doin' the bouncin' thing since," Martin said.

"If you're half as good as your talk, sure, come on up," Ian said.

"Martin, if you've played since a kid, you're probably over-qualified, so for now, no fancy stuff, please," Laney cautioned. "Just lay low and keep it simple. Ian will give you signals. You've heard us play before, so just riff off of what Eddie did."

"What Laney said," Ian said.

"You mean, don't do this?" Martin effortlessly played a

few passages of "Clocks" by Coldplay. The other band members collectively dropped their jaws.

"This gon' be fun," said Martin, folding his fingers outward to crack his knuckles.

Before The Demands started, Laney made a stage announcement.

"Hey, dudes, everybody ready for a good time?" This time tested proclamation caused the expected party roar. It also bought time for the band to finish up their prep.

"Tonight, we have some personnel changes and we hope you like them. They're good guys or I'd kick their asses off the stage, so bear with us if things get wonky." Laney could work a crowd with her innate likability. It didn't hurt that she looked great in the acid green blouse with spaghetti straps. Once the introductions were made, she cued the opening song.

This new version did a respectable job, and both Laney and Greg would joke to the audience after a song went south, making off-the-cuff jokes that made the whole experience more intimate. Ian tossed more than a few zingers that had everybody cracking up.

The addition of Martin offset the precipitousness of Steve's status. Frank couldn't promise he'd be able to keep filling in. He'd promised his wife just a few more gigs.

A few gigs later, The Demands maintained their edge and kept up with the stage theatrics. Fun as it was, Ian hoped in ten years they could cut back on them, for the sake of his knees. This 2.0 version was working out well even if they didn't have a permanent drummer. More venues beyond Allegheny County not only booked them but would set them up in motel rooms. The rooms were usually musty and they'd have to double up in beds, but it was better than another night in the van. Whoever was in Laney's room offered her the bed for her own, in a gesture of chivalry. She took the floor, to be clear that she didn't want preferential treatment. Offers extended to Ohio. Over time, The Silverfish saw them less, and as a result, fewer people hung around and the unpaid bills mounted.

59

Mitch text messaged Jerry DeSantis about performing for a night or two and learned of The Silverfish's debt problems. It had accumulated half a year's worth of overdue rent and it was close to shutting down. With a lot of work, Mitch believed he could make a Save-The-Silverfish benefit an event to remember. Mitch did some of this and did some of that, too. A lot of it. He got the benefit well-publicized and again The Demands hit the mainstream press. This time, it wasn't a mere mention, but a backstory of both the band and The Silverfish. There was even a photo of the group. Greg wasn't happy with the way it turned out, his head appearing mostly in shadow.

Tickets sold out in record time. To make more room, the Silverfish's fire exit in the back was pried open with a chair. This allowed access to a makeshift back porch. Friends and families were fighting over tickets. Couples broke up over not getting tickets.

The day of the event came, with reporters trying to wriggle through the hardcore townie fans. It was standing room only. An unexpected arrival was Arthur Peters, flanked by two bodyguards in casual attire. The bodyguards aggressively cleared a spot in a darkened corner, to avoid the press for a change. Arthur, an unlikely fan of rock music, was sizing up the place.

In a heartbeat, Jerry DeSantis's exuberance turned to discomfort. He knew firsthand that Arthur wasn't the creature of benevolence he'd invented. Jerry squinted his eyes directly at Arthur, which Arthur took as an invitation to meet face-to-face.

"Look, I know full well your plans, and God knows we could use an infusion of more youth culture here, but The Silverfish has been around seventy years. Do what you want, but maybe we can work something out to keep my family establishment where it is. As it is, The Silverfish is already the lynchpin of this town, far as bringing in steady customers. Where's the harm? We can figure out something together."

"Yeah, but you're you and I'm me. You'll never be me."

"Oh, that's a relief."

"How much would it take for you make a very comfortable early retirement?"

"I don't intend to retire. My kids show no interest, so I'm staying here until I find someone who cares enough to keep it going. Or I'll die tending the bar."

"Here I'm trying to be nice and you're playing hardball. If it's a negotiation tactic, I'm personally insulted."

"You just don't get it, do you, Peters? See all those kids here? This town obviously wants The Silverfish to stay. It's had hard times, but we'll get through this without you."

"You're old enough to understand what eminent domain means. I have enough friends on retainer who are well-versed in eminent domain law."

Jerry dipped his head down, the bald spot on his white hair reflecting in the light. All these good people came out to support him, and in the end, it will have meant nothing.

Keenan was the new bouncer on duty, replacing Johnny, who preferred the drifter's life where he didn't have to answer to anybody. Keenan's eyes focused on Jerry and Arthur. He was hoping Arthur or his wads would try to get physical, and he was coiled like a spring. But Jerry walked away untouched. Keenan saw this kind old man take a beatdown with only words and was appalled. Knowing he could do nothing, he focused on the task at hand, looking for other troublemakers.

60

The band was set up and various pre-show music rumblings were heard. By now, The Demands had incorporated a curtain to separate them from the audience until show time.

To everyone's elation, Steve showed up early and ready to rock. All the attention from the Save the Silverfish concert must have appealed to his vanity. This was going to be Frank's last night anyway. He'd be missed, but he'd chosen his road and The Demands chose theirs.

Greg gave Steve a nod of acknowledgement.

"Hey hey hey now, don't start no drumstick tossin' tonight, got it?"

"Don't be a dickhead and the sticks will remain in their holsters."

They shared devilish stares before taking their places. Greg cleared his throat several times, and hocked a loogie on the stage.

"Paul, remember, key change on the final chorus."

"I don't require adult supervision, okay?"

Ian was sick of the Sisyphus role thrust upon him, and this was not lost on Mitch. Ian had gotten Laney up to speed, but Paul seemed a lost cause. Paul was still an uneven player. He proved he could rip out killer sounds and wild improvisations, but other nights, he'd revert to type. There were two Pauls.

Mitch pulled him aside.

"Now don't get freaked out, but I saw Marnie out there."

"Really? Maybe I should go see—"

"Listen to me, listen to me. When that curtain goes up, don't look around, don't stare. How many times has she burned you before? You told me, that even after your divorce, she'd work you and fuck with your head. She's not done playin' you, and I guaran-goddamn-tee that she'll play you again tonight. If you let her. Show her what's she's missing out on, you can do this."

Mitch gathered the other band members and gave a sermon on the mount speech about how tonight they'd make magic and be that much closer to national exposure.

When the curtains parted, a thrumming noise slowly built while Ian did the four-count. Then music that could only be described as angry, yet melodic white noise plowed relentlessly through the core of the attendees. Paul was at the height of his guitar prowess, putting on a spectacular assortment of fireworks that punctuated the songs at just the right spots. The rest of the band, inspired, took turns, tossing in unrehearsed free-form fills. It was an exuberant shared experience. The crowd's shrieks and shouts were drowned out by the onslaught of the opening number. The Silverfish's windows rattled.

As the final notes wrapped up the show, The Demands received the longest applause they'd ever heard. Sweat rolled off their noses and soaked their clothes completely. A shirtless Greg had his face buried in a towel. Steve fell asleep on his drum kit. Martin closed his eyes, and smiled, making a silent prayer of gratitude. A wiped out Ian clumsily wrapped a drenched arm around a similarly drenched Paul. Laney lay on the floor, as if she were making sweat angels. She stared at the small, multicolored canned lights above, completely spent. It was the music festival all over again.

•   •   •

The band was filled with merriment. Back slapping, cracking wise and everything was coming up unicorns. Mitch would have to add unicorns in The Demands' rider someday.

"Mitch! Do—do you think Marnie saw me kickin' ass tonight?"

"Nah."

"What do you—?"

"I was just jaggin' you. She never was here, as far as I know. I rolled the dice that you would either choke or put on the performance of your life, and you totally nailed it, my friend!"

Paul nailed Mitch in the gut with his fist. Then he walked away. Mitch balled up on the floor, gasping for air he thought would never come. Laney and Ian collected themselves to join Mitch. Even Greg raced to Mitch's side.

Martin picked Mitch up and cradled him.

"You okay, son?"

Mitch was relearning how to breathe. "Ohhhhh." His voice trailed off.

The benefit concert exceeded expectations and raised all the money owed and more. Now more national acts showed up to try out new set lists before starting tours in support of new albums. It looked like The Silverfish was going to remain a staple in Tungsten Heights.

Mitch now needed an intern. Her name was Mary, a plus-size business undergrad, who Mitch could rely on to field all the offers. One of Mitch's ships came in. The crowdfunder he started met its goals so he could produce some exclusive merch and private access to the band at gigs. The private access could be had for free if they just wandered enough bars in Pittsburgh, but why volunteer that? Mary placed the orders for the t-shirts with the logo Mitch designed. Twice the amount of XXL than the other sizes. These were a one-time production and future shirts would have different looks entirely. That way, the early fans could have bragging rights. There were other giveaways as well. More importantly, Mitch could give the band members a nice hunk of change.

61

Greg ran into Steve at an art gallery opening. These were the best places to both socialize with the artsy scene and glom free snacks and drink. The drunker they got, the louder they talked. The well-dressed and the self-made-clothes crowd gave them both the stink eye.

"Again, sorry for being a dick sometimes . . ." said Steve.

"Ain't nothin' but a thing. Consider it over!"

"On a more salient topic, I'm soooo sick o' takin' orders from some lil' brat who ain't even from here!" Steve said.

"Yeah, and Ian goes along with her. Maybe he wants a piece if he ain't already getting' it."

"That fucker Mitch, too! I'd love to throw him through a window. And I don't mean that motherfuckin' sugar glass they use in the movies, either!"

Greg and Steve cracked themselves up. Steve was gagging and grasping for air.

When reprimanded by the host, Greg got belligerent and caused a ruckus. Two security guards walked towards Greg. One tall and heavy, one slight and wiry.

"A'right! The cast of *Tommy Boy* showed up!" laughed Greg.

As the guards skittered towards them, Greg and Steve ran out the door in opposite directions, laughing the whole time. The guards stopped at the entrance. Their job was to lose troublemakers, not arrest them.

Amongst the faddish at the gallery was Todd Krupin. He'd

known Greg for some time, but wasn't recognized, thankfully. Imagine the embarrassment if Greg came up to him in public, making an ass of himself. Usually, Greg was Mr. Smooth when he scored.

Steve ran as hard as he could, wheezing the whole time. A few blocks later, he found a bar and entered, doing his best to act casual. He held in his gasps for air, the way a child does when playing hide-and-seek. Keep cool. He staggered to the men's restroom and locked the door behind him. Confident he was hidden, he lay down. His head was heavy and on the filthy tile floor he fell into a deep sleep.

62

The Demands graduated to better clubs. Ian was joyous to have made it to Hologram, voted Best Music Club three years in a row by the *Freeloader*. He'd seen great acts here, in their pupation state before going national.

It was evident that Steve wasn't coming tonight. The benefit show had built up false hope. His vices had been impairing his abilities, and Laney conceded that he was out of the band. Frank was contacted again, but his mind was made up, his family came first. But he knew other drummers he could recommend. Sure enough, a 5'3" bulky fireplug named Jason Bielicki, showed up, elated to play with The Demands. At Hologram! He was too heavy for his height, but, as with Steve's teeth, behind the drums, who could tell?

Greg's clove cigarette, combined with his cologne was a putrid smell. It was his Do Not Disturb sign.

A tall, ginger-haired man who looked college age and probably clocked in at 300 pounds, got uncomfortably into Greg's personal space.

"Sir, this establishment is a smoke-free environment. You'll have to put it out."

"I'm the talent, which means I get a pass. I see that fat fuck over there puffin' away at his stogie! Tell him first, then get back to me."

"Who do you think you are, runt?"

"See that band setup over there? My band. I call the shots."

"Look, I'm going to tell you one more time. Lose the cig!"

"If you insist." Greg contemptuously flung his cigarette down, where it bounced off Ginger's shoe before it hit the floor. Greg stepped on it.

Ginger kept his cool and walked away. The way they'd taught him in anger-management class.

"We're on in five!" Ian shouted across the room.

Various noises came from the stage as The Demands readied their instruments. The guitars and keyboard were being tuned up. Jason tightened the drums and did some paradiddle action. The "test, test, check, check" of the mic by one of the roadies. Martin reread passages from *The Art of War* to psyche himself out.

The din of randomness began to take shape as Greg finally took the stage. He had been waiting until the right moment. He was a handful, but he did know how to make an entrance.

The band was loud, confident and comfortable as a group.

The final set began with a riotous, ballsy song that got people back on their feet. Maybe it was the vodka, but Mitch thought all the stars were finally in alignment.

"Hey!" yelled a beautiful brunette in Mitch's direction.

"Hey yourself!" Mitch yelled back. She walked slowly until she leaned right next to Mitch. She radiated the scent of jasmine. Even under low lights, he could tell her skin was a perfect golden tone. Mitch would swear on a pallet of bibles he had never witnessed such beauty before.

"You're him, aren't you?"

Whaa-runnnnng!

"You really the manager of The Demands?"

"You're lookin' at him!"

Whack-akk! Tish! Tish!

"Havin' a good time, sounds like!"

"What? I'm having trouble hearing you?"

"I said, do you want to make out?"

That he heard.

"Come with me, my voice is raw from shouting!" The girl led Mitch by the hand.

Mitch and the mystery girl left, passing some wasted dude, who gave a thumbs-up.

The two strolled down the alley. The rush of cool air added to his titillation.

Further down the alley, away from the club, a lone street lamp gave Mitch and the girl deep, romantic shadows, the kind seen in old black-and-white movies. She leaned coquettishly against a pearl-white Cadillac, her smile inviting. Mitch scooted nose-to-nose with her.

"Mmm. Now I smell something else sweet," Mitch said.

"I like my mojitos. Wanna taste?"

Mitch and his new paramour kissed a kiss that never seemed to end.

"You! Off the car! I just had it detailed!"

Mitch and the girl disengaged the liplock to see Hologram's silent partner, Arthur Peters, bookcased by two bodyguards, a stubblehead and a lumbersexual, who both towered over Mitch. The girl hop-skipped away from Mitch to rest her head against the stubblehead.

"Don't pout, hon. I had to be convincing, didn't I? Call me when you're off the clock, 'kay?"

"Oh, it's my good friend who saved the Silverfish. I was hopin' to have a sit-down wi' you eventually, but clearly you have already formed your opinions about me, calling me a, what'd he call me, boys?"

"Eh, a . . . a . . . fat fuck, sir."

"After all those times I let your little band of merry men get your start at my clubs."

Mitch, not knowing the source of Arthur's discontent, trembled.

"Look, I get the drill! It's ninth grade all over again! If you really want, I'll get on my knees and call myself a crybaby bitch! With real tears! I'll really sell it! Just tell me why you're doing this!"

"I'm afraid we're past that stage, Mr . . . Shaler, right?

Now was not a good time to correct him.

"Give my good friend here a lesson in manners. Do damage, but no broken bones, got it? Save that for future conversations." There was no attempt to reason at this point. A world of pain was heading towards Mitch, so he saw no shame in trying to squirrel though the muscle men. Stubblehead clotheslined him, which flipped Mitch back to hit the pavement. Hard. Next to Arthur's feet.

"Oh God!" He faced the street, just a few yards away. It may as well have been miles away.

"Hey! Some help here!"

"Scream your head off if it'll make you feel better. No one will hear you over that shit you call music."

Arthur turned to Mitch as he cracked open Hologram's door, just enough to keep Mitch out of view of the crowd inside. Then the door shut with a vault-like sound. Mitch's head was still reeling from the clothesline but he managed to find purchase from the wall to stand. Lumbersexual flexed his muscles, then sauntered towards Mitch.

"Look, I got called in on my night off, so let's just get this thing done, hah?" he said in a matter-of-fact way.

Lumbersexual squeezed Mitch by both ears, before pulling Mitch's face down to meet his uplifted knee square on. In the trade, it's called a Stop Sign. Mitch's limp body tossed back. A trail of blood danced out his nose, before Mitch dropped again to the pavement. He lay there for a time, among garbage, empty beer cases and leaflets that promoted The Demands' appearance at Hologram.

"Mitch! Mitch!" Ian screamed, seeing Mitch rising on one knee, with his face down.

"Where the hell have you been? Are you wasted? Need me to call an ambulance?"

"Nu-nung. Banged up, suckered." Mitch was now sitting, with one hand holding his head, still face down.

"This is getting to be a habit," Ian said, his attempt at levity. "Laney told me you did a vanishing act."

Then Mitch's head raised. Ian gasped at seeing his cousin's face, battered and bloodied.

"That's it! We're getting you to a hospital!"

Mitch woozily nodded.

"Then we're making a police report."

Mitch, through sheer tyranny of will, regained his senses though the fog of pain enough to stare Ian squarely in the eye.

"You do that . . . and you and me are through."

"What?"

"I mean it, I mean it. I got this."

"What the hell do you mean 'I got this'? You got your ass handed to you, that's what you got!"

Mitch's eyes were now capable of opening fully as he

stared down Ian again, laying his bloody hand on Ian's best shirt.

"I mean it as much as I ever meant anything in my life. I got this. Nobody does a thing about this. I'll . . . manage . . . just fine. That's wha' managers do, right?"

Ian was incensed. He helped Mitch shuffle back into the club, looking for Arthur, who was gone by then.

Laney saw two figures backlit in the doorway and it immediately registered who they were. She raced over to their side. Laney cried out in horror.

"Who did this to you?"

"Manager Mitch isn't taking any questions at this time," Ian said angrily.

"What happened? You disappeared when that slut showed up. Why, Mitch, why?" Laney's eyes grew red and fierce, as she slammed her fists on his chest, bumping him against the door.

"You're supposed to look after *us*, goddamn you! You tell us—" Her hands now pointed at herself, for emphasis. "—the troops, right? To give our all, and you pull this shit on us now, just when things are happening?"

"I got nothin'. I fucked up, I know. But I think we can all agree tha' I learned a big lesson today. You can stay pissed at me or we can move on."

"I can't take this!" Laney was out the door before anyone could dissuade her.

Mitch careened to the bar and ordered a double vodka. His lip still bled despite a quick washing up in the men's room. His vodka began to turn pink, then red. He drank it anyway.

63

Ian didn't talk to Mitch for days. Finally, the tension of not speaking got the best of him and he called Mitch to ream him out. Mitch had no defense and took his reaming. Then Ian spent the following week cajoling Laney for hours to forgive Mitch.

She passed the time busking in the strip district. The strip district was a long one-way street mostly populated by Old World immigrants. They ran bakeries, sold rare spices and plenty of cheese. The smells were intoxicating. Street vendors with Steelers knock-off merch, trucks delivering fresh fish. All the exotic pedestrian traffic provided the perfect backdrop for Laney. She made just enough money daily for a sit-down dinner, but it was neat, winning crowds over by herself. The best day was when the dancing pizza-sign guy broke it down for her while she played. She had softened up to a point when Ian's tenacious phone calls and texts, with carefully-chosen words, eventually swayed her to give Mitch another chance.

64

Another week later, at Ian's apartment, tempers cooled, as emotions had been drained. The band's future was less predictable than a shattered Magic 8 ball. Laney slapped a cigarette from Greg's hand before he could light it, almost a form of play between them. He may have been a drama queen, but he cared deeply about the band making it, more than his cool façade let on. Steve was absent once more. Hopefully he wasn't going to show up announcing he'd be a father. Mitch's nose was stuffed with gauze with tape to keep it in place. Some cartilage in his nose needed to be drilled so he could eventually breathe through it again. Mitch's cell rang. Mitch did his best to hide his damaged nasal voice over his cell phone.

"Uh huh. I see. Therr outta town. Ma name's Mitch Shlayter. No, no, it's ess-el-ay-tee-arr. A fred'. I be there shortly."

"Who was that? Steve?" said Laney.

"Lady o' Grace Hosbital. S-steve's dead."

65

"There was an inordinate amount of codeine, prometha-zine and alcohol in his system," the attending physician told the band.

"The street term for it is Lean. Also Purple Drank. It's been a recent problem for partiers. Cough syrup is the main ingredient, and the prescription strength is most desirable. For flavor, they mix in some pop. The user gets stimulated while experiencing a state of euphoria. But after continuous usage, it continues to slow your breathing down. Your friend most likely died of cumulative respiratory failure, cardiac arrest. I'm very sorry."

"S-s-teve's parents are semi-retired in Arizona. I tink we shu' dummy up for now until they arrive."

Laney slumped in a chair, her hands covering her face.

"My head hurts so much. It's throbbing."

"Laney . . ."

"No. no." Now she was twinging.

"Just remembered. He . . . never *did* return that cough syr-up I gave him."

Ian put a hand on her shoulder.

"He would have gotten it one way or another. Don't—"

"And please stop talking. And let go. Every sound hurts my head more. My brain tells me that, but . . . shit, I don't know."

Greg blew his nose with a tissue to hide his tears. For all he knew he was the last one to have seen Steve alive.

• • •

Ian took Mitch aside in the hallway.

"Is this how it ends? You rope me into your pie-in-the-sky dream of big time. And now your nose is broke and Steve is dead. I may have hated my old job but nobody got hurt."

"S-steve was an accident wading to happen, an' you know it. Az for me, ahm willing to carry on."

"This discussion is not over," Ian whispered as the rest of the band approached.

They all took defensive postures, arms folded or hands in pockets, and looking away from each other.

"So *now* what?" Ian said.

"I don't know about you guys, but I didn't come all the way from Maryland to quit."

"Maybe we should have a group meeting about this. Not a practice. Just air out our grievances," Martin said.

"Not for me. I don't have time for my real friends any-more," Paul complained.

Laney, with one hand on a temple, mustered the courage to expand on her feelings about Steve. Her voice dropped, unbelievably low.

"When Steve was down or strung out, I made the usual noises: 'Oh, you're a great guy to work with, so much to live for . . .' I pegged Steve as the kind of guy who simply liked to hear such things and it wouldn't change his behavior a bit. I could only play counsellor so long. So I . . . cut him loose. I failed him."

"You can't say you didn't try. We all failed him. God rest his soul," Martin said.

Greg just listened, hoping God did rest his soul.

66

Arthur knew his sophomore effort had to be at least as successful as Turnbul. He didn't want to be some damn footnote, embossed on a postcard-sized plaque in a rinky-dink museum of Pittsburgh beneficiaries. He was putting extra pressure on himself, and it was building at an alarming rate. The diet the wife put him on he didn't need now on top of everything. His weight kept fluctuating, which compounded his feelings of inadequacy. He'd made more money than he'd thought possible, but financial gain wasn't enough at this point. This was to be his legacy. He no longer trusted anybody enough, neither family or subordinates, to confide in. Even Texas hold-'em with the local elite wasn't the release it once was. He even considered talking to Bishop Alexie about the wall he'd built around himself. But after that one phone call when he offered a new church for Alexie's holy support, no.

If he wasn't going to be promoted by his mob overseers, by God, he was going to own Pittsburgh. He *could* parlay his stature into a political office. He liked all the attention, but he was a hands-on man. Better to be a beloved benevolent figurehead than a boring, detached lawmaker. Staying where he was, he'd be under less scrutiny. That didn't mean he couldn't hire lobbyists. Many of them were up-and-comer politicians or former politicians, well versed in making deals with the devil. More specifically, other devils.

He held another fund-raiser of his own in the Hyatt's

main ballroom. Only the best food was served. The prime rib got the most compliments. His upper-crust guests denigrated The Silverfish and the crowd it attracted. Arthur was more the karaoke type, and reassured them that he would give this landmark a makeover. Maybe turn it into a state-of-the-art sports bar.

67

Laney lay on the bed belly-down, kicking her feet up, back and forth. Watching crappy sitcoms on her secondhand TV. She wasn't up to sharing any thoughts on social media. There was an emptiness she couldn't shake since Steve's death.

A rapid knock on Laney's door shook her out of her zombie-state.

It was Todd.

"Laney, I know you're mad at me, but I had to come over to see how you're doing since Steve died. I just wanted you to know that if you need a shoulder to cry on, I'm here for you."

"I'm good. Really."

"Shit, what a way to go. Can't imagine his last moments, alone in some stinkin' bathroom."

Laney backed away from him.

"Waitaminnit! How did *you* know where he was found? No one knows about Steve except his parents and the band!"

"Shh! Margo might hear you!"

"This just gets better. You know Margo's here? Nobody knows Margo except me . . ."

She counted by holding down her index finger.

"Vic," she said, holding down the middle finger. "And Blackie," she said, holding down three fingers.

"Laney, it looks bad on paper, but—"

"Out."

"Bu—"

"You don't leave now, you'll have six people carrying you by the handles!"

He complied. Then she took phone in hand.

"Ian. I'm not ready to scrub the mission."

68

By now, Turnbul was on autopilot so Arthur could invest his time, and other's money, into Tungsten Heights. Nonetheless, there were setbacks aplenty. Tungsten Height's code enforcement officer was a newly promoted assiduous young man with something to prove. He took his new post seriously and didn't take a liking to Arthur's bullying tactics or bribes. Not long ago, Arthur could have ended his existence with little effort, but it was too risky now. A mysterious loss of a government official entrusted to approve Arthur's proposals would make it too easy for anyone to connect the dots. There were other misfortunes, and they were growing. His sheen had begun to dull. But it wouldn't do well if Arthur allowed his declining composure to show in public.

Also he'd made the mistake of outsourcing construction for Tungsten Heights, hoping to pass the savings onto himself. The local teamsters didn't care for that at all. Verbal and physical disputes increased. An outspoken union leader got the stray on-the-take members who answered to Peters permanently expelled. This same union leader united the media to the Teamster Temple, getting the word out that Arthur Peters used illegal loopholes in the creation of his Peters Foundation. The Foundation extended his workforce to his special interest firms, with no competing contractor bids per law. He called Arthur out and the media pivoted its collective head as a serpent would to Arthur Peters. The results were several badly blundered media attempts to save face, which became that week's meme sensations. Things were so much simpler when you could control the source with kickbacks. Now everybody had camera phones.

He hadn't factored this in. More than ever, he became self-conscious to maintain levelheadedness. He popped more anti-depressants than his doctors prescribed, washing them down with booze. He expected this second time at the bat to be arduous, but it was far more than he expected. He was in too deep to stop. Once he'd succeeded in making a second rat-hole town an upscale one, even more doors would open. The template would then be set and he could ride out the wave from there on. Let go of the daily duties and hand pick honest movers and dishonest shakers. Sit back, relax, and become a fixture in Pittsburgh's rich history, just like *Mr. Rogers' Neighborhood*.

His closest soldiers and adult children were all over town supervising personnel, contracts, and brick and mortar needs for Turnbul. They tried talking Arthur out of undercutting the unions on Tungsten Heights, but his ego had final say. The siblings were busily repairing this gaffe. They circled the wagons and adroitly placated some critics with feigned ignorance, expertly learned from their friends in Washington. Even their course correcting efforts couldn't mask the snafu of shutting out the unions. The Pittsburgh area was the wrong place to screw with unions. The Teamsters won the battle and got the contracts to build Tungsten Heights.

69

The following week, there was a press conference held by Kiesha Gaines, a fashion-forward woman with wine-dark ring-lets of hair and trendy eyeglasses. She had called the press to publicly resign as one of the Peters Foundation's board members. She had discovered that there were creative accounting practices that not only bordered on illegal, but were outright cause for criminal investigation.

Rather than put her reputation at stake, she became a whistle-blower with a lot to say. She apologized to those who'd donated money that could have gone to the underprivileged. She found that a percentage of the donations went to Arthur's private slush fund. This slush fund was funneled to offshore accounts. She'd backed up her accusations with evidence presented to the press. She knew that going public would cost her a job, but she hadn't joined the foundation to exploit others.

She didn't speak of Arthur's ties to the Russian mob, as that hadn't been proven yet and she'd be subject to slander. There were enough nails in the coffin of the Peters Foundation as it was. Local news stations interrupted scheduled programming to cover the press conference.

"I have spoken to a considerable number of charities that had become associated with the Peters Foundation, and they will make upcoming statements renouncing all ties with the Foundation. Moreover, they have agreed to appoint me head of the upcoming Save Our Burgh Humanitarian Project,

pending investigations. These charities have been hand selected as the very best to repair broken promises from us to you."

When confronted by the flurry of questions she had daz-
zled the crowd with her plain-speaking ways. Her graceful
candor enamored the media during this maiden public outing.
There was a new sheriff in town.

70

Arthur's outward appearance was deteriorating and his impatience reached a boiling point at times. As a result, his influence was waning. His media insiders no longer returned calls. And they weren't the only ones. Emails bounced back. His allies' administrative assistants, once eager to expedite contacts, were ordered not to respond. The new associates he'd culled in the past year blanched when they'd run into him in person. The collection of withdrawn promises grew. "Maybe the next project, as we've met our budget for the quarter." "Wish we had something to contribute, but we've just backed another costly project" "I will keep you in mind at the next meeting of the shareholders." "Times are tight and we're stretched thin as is." "Things are crazy at the moment, but you'll be notified, when the smoke clears." They began looking away from Arthur the way they would a chewed piece of gum on a urinal cake.

The wife had left for an extended vacation in Europe, with no set date for return. The mistress offered to stick around until he got up on his feet again. He refused and she left for parts unknown. Forever, if the pros did their work with their usual finesse. His adult children stayed by his side. They knew where their potato bread was buttered. Todd, his usual clueless self, imagined new ideas for Tungsten Heights.

Given enough time, Arthur could concoct a narrative that he, too, would be a whistle-blower, blaming his board of trustees for the mismanagement of the Peters Foundation. Until the promising young lobbyist Arthur had backed out, switching allegiance to advance his political aspirations. Exposing the Peters Foundation's shell game was the crusade he built his new platform on, for an electorate eager for change. Municipalities pulled back support, as they were now under federal scrutiny.

All the work required to establish his foolish empire was too daunting for Arthur now. To nullify accusations from the rabble, then revisit the hardships of rebuilding would be the death of him. The epicenter of his manhood was his work ethic, his gifts for making money, now robbed of him by age and poor health. In this new era, the business model that defined him was now crumbling and obsolescent. He needed some time off to regenerate and rethink his life. If the end was near, he would leave and live life to the fullest.

The Silverfish was still a sore spot to him. It had gotten a lot of attention, and started the ball rolling on his negative publicity. The Demands were declared heroes for saving the Silverfish. The 70-year-old eyesore, which had been prepared for the wrecking ball, was now declared an official landmark. This perturbed Arthur to no end, to be undone by those unseemly lowlife punks.

Strip clubs offered the same old pleasures to Arthur, but he'd had his fill of the same old same old. Whether by depleted hormones or endless self-medication, sex no longer held the allure it once had. The money-fueled adoration was always welcome, but if there was no more lead in his pencil, what did it matter? He needed something, anything, to clear his mind. Movies couldn't hold his attention and gambling probably wasn't the best idea in his current state. Maybe that idiot Todd would know a place in town to lay low and have fun.

71

"Is this Mitch Slater?" the voice on the phone said.

"Speaking."

"Could you come and get your friend? He was dropped off here at the emergency room and he has traces of heroin and alcohol in his system. His only form of ID was your business card."

Greg hadn't thrown out the business card after all. Mitch wrestled his jacket on, inventing new curse words as he charged out the door. But he was not going to fail Greg the way he had Steve.

Mitch showed up alone. He was met by a tall, burly paramedic with tattoo sleeves. After Mitch showed his ID and gave Greg's description, he was taken to a curtained-off hospital bed. Greg was naked, his foul-smelling clothes in a toxic waste bin. A Jamaican woman was washing away vomit, feces and piss while prying Greg from his fetal position.

"Someone called this in, and we got there just in time. Your friend was barely breathing, turning blue. We administered two milligrams of Narcan, just enough to wake him up. Narcan blocks the narcotic receptors for heroin. You have to introduce it gradually. For a skinny dude, he's pretty strong. Had to restrain his arms and legs on the ambulance bed once the Narcan kicked in and woke him up. Guess he just wore himself out, struggling. But he's stable for now."

"This must be pretty routine for you."

"I'd like to say no, but I see this every day. We do what we can, but unless we're notified, it can mean the end for the victim."

"Thank you for rescuing him. Any idea who called it in?"

"Not yet, but our first priority is saving the victim."

The paramedic's radio squawked. The dispatcher placed another emergency.

"I'm on it," the paramedic replied. "I have to go now, but good luck. The next week is going to be rough for him, going through the DTs. He needs someone to watch over him 24/7. Take care, sir."

"Thanks again."

He'd seen Greg fucked up many a time, but never in a helpless state. The Jamaican nurse fought back Greg's renewed resistance, dressed him in a gown then attached a Narcan drip with astonishing speed. A rigorous task well handled in a nurturing, calm fashion. For her this was just another Tuesday.

The Narcan did its job again. Greg's eyes were open, but he was in a state of delirium. Eventually his dosage was doubled to the point where he was more lucid. Mitch scooted a chair next to Greg. Nothing was said for some time.

"What happened, Greg?"

"My lady. She put me out."

"At the risk of getting all Doctor Phil on you, wanna talk about it?"

"Not much to say. Fuck me, this is embarrassing."

Greg eyes were glued to the potted textures in the ceiling tiles. It was now the most interesting thing Greg saw in his life.

"Don't tell me you're surprised. Been on before I knew you, so this's old hat. The stuff must not have been cut enough.

Maybe he thought he was doin' me a favor."

"I don't see any needle marks."

"What am I, an imbecile? There's lots of places, between your toes, lots o' places. Wanna know?"

"Heh. No, Greg. Who did this to you?"

"Ehhhhh. Just some fucker. A fucker I need to see right now."

"Uh, in college I got wasted more than a few times. I got put off after some laced—"

"Trying to relate with me? Here comes the sponsor speech."

"Yeah, well, I'm here and your dealer friend's not." Greg turned his head to the left side of his bed, looking at the Narcan drip.

"I'm sick of being taken for granted. I may be quirky and needy but I support this band with every erg of my being. Sure, I can be a pain in the ass, but that's me and I don't see any change in that. I feel cut off and dismissed just for being me. You ain't been what I been through. Some things I'll never tell another soul."

"Fair enough."

Another nurse intruded on the conversation.

"Mr. Burdette, you're free to go."

Greg stood up on his own. "Good. I wasn't keen on giving a free show of my ass. Gotta pay if you want some'a this." He slapped his ass in front of the nurse.

"That's it? What do we do now?"

"Pick up some clothes from my lady's place, I guess, and lose this gown."

It was going to be a long week.

72

Mitch already had a lot on his plate. The Demands' currency with the public was still strong, and he'd mapped out things for the rest of the week.

Pain in the ass, Mitch thought. What a hateful thing to think. Greg almost died alone. The weight of the situation caused Mitch to take a step back and remember why he began managing the band. To look out for their best interests, but he'd sold them short, only focusing on the financial and the promotional.

The paramedic told him to keep an eye on Greg. That translated to *Keep Greg from scoring again.*

Mitch's first impulse was to bring in Ian and Laney, but given Greg's personality, it could most likely backfire. Instead of explaining the situation, he texted a brief message that he was going to be away for some time, incommunicado. The text could very well mean he was going to really lose his job. But, just like his job at Devinshire Concepts, it didn't matter in the big scheme of things. Seeing Greg in such a state made Mitch feel shameful. All this time he'd treated the band members like cogs in a machine. A better manager would have taken a proactive move by addressing Steve's and Greg's problems before they got out of hand. He didn't even like Greg, but was now responsible to help him help himself. Mitch was reminded of all the times his mother had taken in sick relatives she knew weren't ever going to get better. No one could ask for a better caregiver on their deathbed. And Rose was not the healthiest person either, but she went the distance to give others comfort in their final days. She was better equipped to deal with this sort of thing, but just handing Greg over to her would be callous and cruel. She'd done more than her share and it was his turn.

Maybe this was the reason Mitch's life was saved by Dr. Shim.

He powered off his phone and kept it hidden for as long as Greg needed him. Greg was too worn out to resist crashing at Mitch's place. Greg had to stay put, so it meant Mitch staying put. Mitch had zero experience about helping someone wean himself off heroin. Weaning off the meds Mitch experienced in the hospital was nothing close to this. Even if there was an instruction manual, there was no one-size-fits-all solution.

73

Day one was spent watching old movies. Greg smoked like a demon, which stung Mitch's eyes at times in close quarters. Greg had no appetite. He just gazed at the TV, going through one cigarette after another. He'd rap the bottom of the cigarette pack at least 20 times even though one would pop out after two whacks. Mitch was less than thrilled to honor Greg's request for a few cartons of cigarettes when they picked up his clothes, but if it meant keeping Greg near, it was a necessary evil.

Day two, shakes and abdominal cramps came and went. Greg said he was fine and ready to leave. Mitch wasn't having it. Greg wasn't one for being told what to do. Voices raised until Mitch had to physically restrain Greg, which wasn't easy. Several other wrestling escape attempts were attempted. Mitch was surprised that none of his neighbors called the cops when Greg would scream for help.

Greg was breaking down, and Mitch wasn't far behind. Mitch became a sleep deprived guard watching Greg sleep solidly for hours at a time. Mitch's eyes drooped and he started to pass out until he heard uncontrollable crying. Greg was inconsolable. Once he'd worn himself out crying, he'd curl up in the bed with a pillow over his face. Mitch had heard many accounts of someone going through the DTs but witnessing it firsthand bordered on ghoulish.

•   •   •

Greg propped himself up on the bed, wincing, his back hurting from lying down so much. Seeing that the sunlight was agonizing Greg, Mitch closed all the blinds and lowered the lights. Greg lit up a cigarette, his wakeup ritual.

"I'll be already. Alright, I mean. Just call my friend, you c'n trust 'im. He's taken good care'a me, don't worry. C'mon, fucker, just do it, 'kay? I'm fine."

"What will make you fine is getting some food in you. You haven't eaten in days. And you weren't exactly husky before." That sounded like something Mitch would hear his mother say.

"Not hungry. Just let me die, a'ight?" Greg said as Mitch studied his withered arms.

Mitch was tempted to comply. Then off himself to end his misery, too. Mitch felt like he was falling apart. In advertising and promotion, he'd excelled at being a champion bullshit artist. But he never imagined he'd be in the position of saving the life of another champion bullshit artist. They just had different skill sets.

One pot of coffee after another was chugged day and night to fight off Mitch's sleep-deprived delirium. Maybe he'd only need a few more days, maybe maybe. Tattoo guy at the hospital said a week was all that's needed to wean him. Week doesn't mean a calendar week. Stupid. He wasn't getting clean seven days to the minute after he got in the ambulance.

Eventually, Mitch passed out. When he woke up, to his surprise, Greg was still there, asleep. Mitch shook himself awake and poured the still-burning coffee reduction into his smiley face mug. Then he brewed a new pot.

When Greg woke up, his shakes started up again, but not as severe as before. He got up and walked to the stool by the mini-kitchen, waving his hand in a "me, too" gesture. Mitch poured Greg a cup. Then another. Not a word was said. Greg lit up the first cig of the day and drew deep. They were both uncomfortably studying everything in the room but each other. Greg pointed at the donut box by the microwave.

"Anything in there?"

"Sure," said Mitch as he brought the box to Greg. Mitch was careful not to come off as chipper or trite.

Hours passed as Greg drank more coffee and ate. Then he threw up by eating too much too fast. Mitch made no fuss over it, even though his mom had bought him that throw rug years ago when he got his first apartment. Mitch had learned from the Jamaican nurse how to handle such situations in a matter-of-fact manner. More smoking and coffee drinking. Mitch bummed a cig off Greg, a reminder of his college days. Greg slouched back, looking skyward.

"You think it's easy being me, don't you? Mr. Carefree, on the mike, ladies and gents.

"You haven't been in my head. Every day I fight off the urge to kill myself. Even before I got into the heavy stuff, I'd wake up and think 'Goddamn, I'm still alive'. Once I'm up and go through the motions I rejoin the human race. But that nagging never leaves. Who cares if I live or die in a hundred years? But I have to go out there and whore myself out as the big dog. People can smell weakness, especially if you wanna make something of yourself. You put on a mask that everything is fine, but inside you're ready to crumble and feel worthless. Once the high of being celebrated ends, you keep the façade that you're the shit. Deep down, you know you have no intrinsic value. The ones who hammer nails into sheetrock, they have a clear value. You keep your game face on, when you want to just vanish. It's a crapshoot to make it creatively. If I'm lucky, I'll be 'critically acclaimed', y'know—"

He turned from the ceiling to Mitch.

"—the way you get after you die broke."

Mitch kept his mouth shut while Greg went on and on.

74

The Demands were a no-show for a well-paying gig. In Mitch's absence, they didn't know they were booked for it. With Steve, Greg and now Mitch gone, the situation was getting too out of hand for their liking. Maybe the show didn't always necessarily have to go on. Jason still had his day job, as his status was still auxiliary member. Ian even checked about his code-writing job. He'd been replaced. Three times. It was still a heinous company it seemed. Paul spent time with old friends in Homestead. Laney took the losses personally. She was losing control. Maybe she'd move back to Maryland, get married, pop out a few kids and give up. Hand her albums to her grandchildren someday. But she'd be returning a pathetic failure, and that was a deep well from which she'd never escape.

75

Laney came down from her apartment to the bar. Only Blackie was there. She didn't have much to spare on beer, as she got spoiled by comps at gigs. But she needed someone to talk to who was removed from the situation.

"Where is everybody?" Laney asked.

"There's a veteran celebration tonight at the Rotary Club."

"Just as well." She reached into her duffle bag. Blackie shook his head no.

"It's onna house."

"Thanks."

"That's what I like about you. I know when you say thanks you mean it. Lots of folks say it in a sarcastic tone."

"Thank my dad. Being a military brat, I was taught to say 'Thank you', 'please', 'sir' and 'ma'am' a lot."

"I could tell. Maybe they oughtta bring back the draft, then." Blackie smiled as he rotated the stock of snacks behind the bar.

"I'm facing a crisis of faith. My band is falling apart after all the hours, days, weeks and months we devoted to it. You're gonna laugh, but I used to have a childhood crush on Jack White from The White Stripes. Ever hear of them?"

"I ain't that old. Yeah I know of them."

"First time I saw them perform online, I knew what I wanted to do with my life. But the kids are now all about techno and popstrels. Everything but rock 'n' roll. How do I try to break through the mold and think I have something that—"

Blackie stooped down to eye level with her.

"Listen, I'm over fifty with health problems. Me and my woman live in a semi-detached, living a modest lifestyle running this bar. It's over for me. But you're what, early twenties? That's when you have the most energy. Do something with it and take your shot while you can."

Days passed as Laney texted Ian dozens of times before he texted back. His words read in a surly tone. She replied and texted Paul, Martin and Jason that she was going to the garage and if anyone wanted to come, that was fine. If they didn't want to, that was fine too.

76

She'd approached the garage when Charlotte called out from her glider on the front porch.

"Laney, come on in."

"Hmm?"

"Haven't seen you in a while."

"I'm . . . kinda dressed sloppy. I don't want to mess up your house."

"Nonsense, just us girls. How do you like your coffee?"

"Black. As the lowest nether regions of hell black."

They commiserated for a time. Laney found it refreshing to spend time with her. She usually hung with the guys all the time, having grown up a tomboy. She never felt like she fit in with other girls and their catfights. Life itself offered a cornucopia of drama.

"So, Laney, is Ian coming?"

"I don't know if *anybody* is coming. I had nothin' goin' on and I was sick of seeing the same four walls. Plus I think the ghost of rock 'n' roll past just gave me some good advice."

Charlotte wasn't sure if Laney believed herself to be a medium or was indulging in wordplay.

"So what's the deal with you and Ian? I've never known anybody to have an amicable breakup. I thought they only existed in TV and movies."

"Oh, yeah, about that. It's a bit more complex than you might guess."

"You clearly called me in for a reason, not just to finish the coffee pot."

"Let's say . . . I messed up and I want him back."

Just when Charlotte became interesting to Laney, rumblings from the garage door sounded.

Laney dashed out the front door to see Ian parking the van with Martin outside, making hand signals to help land the beast without taking out a fender. Paul and Jason were already in the garage. Laney found purpose again.

Hours later, the four of them tooled around some old songs, but lacked the initiative to try new sounds. Jason was just happy to be there, until he read the mood of the room. He wasn't officially a full-time member yet, was he? Then again, Ian did pick him up with the others. Just shut up and do what they ask, he thought.

What the hell was Mitch doing? Ian was resigned that they may have to fire his favorite cousin. And their lifetime friendship would end. Mitch had done a lot of legwork to get them where they were, even if they hadn't made it national. Instead of anticipating the inevitable, he lost himself in strumming his acoustic guitar.

"Going to miss seeing Mitch on the regular," Martin said.

"Whatever," Ian said in a barely audible voice.

They were morose but playing together. Even playing badly, it was an experience that transcended the need for conversation.

There were a few knocks on the garage door until Mitch and Greg entered.

"Guess who just showed up, fresh off the apology train," Laney said, very pissed.

"So you have a written statement prepared, Mitch? The kind you whip up when you go full salesman?"

Mitch let it sink in for a few heartbeats.

"I could regale you with stories from the last week but you wouldn't want to hear them. There was a grueling incubation period, if you know what I mean. Steve is gone, but Greg is with us. That's all that needs be said."

The weight of Mitch's words, stripped of hype, gave them chills.

"So, Greg, how do you feel?" Ian said sympathetically.

"Like absolute shit. But I have to stay busy to keep my head straight." Greg groaned.

"I'm sorry about the missed gig," Mitch said in his most conciliatory voice.

"It would have been a good stepping stone, I totally own that. But this is not unfixable. Stupid as it sounds, with the right PR damage control, it can create an air of mystery around the band. With Greg's . . . situation resolved, we can right this ship."

"Now it sounds like you're playin' us," Martin said.

"Here, I am holding two new credit cards that are used exclusively for The Demands, and I've already ordered more merch to sell at shows. I didn't even know if you'd take me back, and I'm deeper in debt than I've ever been, but that's how much credence I've always given you. I'm backing a winner. Greg is all good and ready. And so am I."

"Got some coffee?" Greg said while lighting his trademark ciggy.

77

Arthur, in a bloated state of delirium, was escorted to The Hotseat by his chauffeur and bodyguards. Todd's suggestion. Maybe cheering up Uncle Arthur would earn him more points. Arthur hadn't had much time for The Hotseat since building it. Frankly, he'd forgotten all about it. When Todd approached, it was obvious that Uncle Arthur was already tanked and also oblivious that he was drooling. Arthur gave Todd a big hug that lasted a bit too long. Possibly a sign of approval, something he wasn't accustomed to. Todd spent his life meandering and selling hard drugs as the quickest way to make money. Tungsten Heights was a delusion he still clung to, a chance to prove he wasn't going to be a slacker any more, and earn respect. Arthur was mortified enough that he needed his adult children to save his image. His intake of medicine and alcohol increased. It was an unspoken understanding about how Todd made his living, but Arthur's fuzzy reasoning considered non-prescription hard drugs a stigma. But Todd was feeling full of himself now. Not only had he stepped up to help the family business, but he'd taken out Greg Burdette. Partially to get back at them for the Silverfish fiasco, partially to stick it to Laney.

78

In Charlotte's garage, Greg's voice was better, more intense, than ever. He was now singing from a place of pain. Today's band reunion practice might have ended with a somewhat clumsy dismount, but something was still there.

After rehearsal, Ian was dropping off everybody to their homes. As they reached a few streets shy of Martin's home, the street was blocked by a black sedan.

"Hey, move it, you shit!" Ian said, repeatedly honking his horn.

"Screw this, I'm backing up—"

"Stop! There's someone blocking us from behind!" Jason yelped.

A man in a Gucci suit and Ray-Ban Aviators rapped on Ian's window with an Uzi.

Ian rolled down the window.

"Give me your phones. Now."

The band complied.

"There's another car behind us. You're going to follow it."

Again, they did as instructed.

"We are sorely fucked," Greg said, lighting a cigarette.

Paul waved a hand at the smoke. "If you don't mind, I'd rather not spend my last minutes—ah, fuck it."

Jason seized up. Was this another day at the office for them?

Mitch's second chance in life was short-lived it seemed.

He was curled up on the floor by Ian, using his teeth to open a bag of pretzels.

"Pretzels, anyone? Not much of a last meal, I know."

The bag got passed around with no comment, just a sense of finality.

"Dear heavenly father, we ask that you provide us safe passage, but if this is the end of our time in Man's World, we know it is part of your divine plan."

"Yeah, yeah, body of Christ and all that, here's your pretzel," said Greg.

The cobblestone road made them shake about like freshly-popped corn.

The entourage led them to a place all too familiar to Laney.

"Oh, oh, shit."

"What's 'oh oh shit'?" Ian asked.

"Looks like a strip club. No windows," Greg said.

"If we're being punked, I will most definitely kill someone," Paul stated with balled-up fists.

"It's called The Hotseat," Laney said.

"Where? I don't see any sign, just cars out front."

"Nice cars, too," observed Greg.

"In all my years of playing, I have never once heard of a 'Hotseat'."

"An exclusive club, Ian. Todd used to take me here. It's *America's Got Talent*, angry mob style. Long story."

"Soon to be short," Ian said while putting the van in park.

Ray-Bans ordered the band to exit the van. Martin leaned his head down and gave one of the gunmen a long, hard stare. As a man of God he wanted his captors to know he'd made his peace with his maker.

79

The rear door of a limousine was opened by the driver. A long leg pulled out a willowy, platinum-blond, middle aged, striking woman. Her gown and shawl cost more than the average person's annual income.

"You've become quite the well-known irritant to Artur Petrov," she stated with an odd accent. The same one Todd had. "You know him as Arthur Peters. This is not necessarily a bad thing. It is good for you to be present, to throw his failings in his face. That said, you all know too much."

"Come," she nodded. The gunmen made the band enter first.

"Vasti-ist-fucking-dast?" Greg said.

"Wrong nationality," Laney said, trying to sound brave while pretending this wasn't happening.

80

"Laney! What in the fuck brings you here?" Todd said as he shot out of his chair. Arthur was indignant to see these punks traipsing into his personal clubhouse.

"Get them out of here, I don't care how—" His words clipped short upon seeing the woman follow directly behind the band.

Every head turned towards her.

"All of you, stay where you are!" the woman said in her husky voice.

"Larisa!" Arthur said. Larisa Nevelskoi, the wife of Anatoly Nevelskoi, the head of the mob, east coast.

Arthur's posturing crumpled upon seeing Larisa.

"What a pleasure it is to see you," Arthur said as he reached for her hand to kiss. She pulled her hand away to run a finger through her perfectly coiffed hair.

"I am here to personally clean up your mess. Anatoly wants it known that you, your family and subordinates are now cut loose from the Bratva. Your thirst for attention has ill-served the organization and unnecessarily risked our visibility."

Arthur shed all dignity and bent to his knees. His voice took a mawkish tone.

"You know I would never hold back any earnings from Anatoly. Our revenue increased almost twelve percent since I started the Foundation."

"Dude's completely losing his shit," Greg muttered.

"Arthur. You and yours will leave the country or you will lose your lives. But first I want you to know why you went above your station like a fool. Why do you think Anatoly kept you here all these years? You've overstepped your boundaries and made a spectacle of yourself publicly. Greedy and sloppy. How could you have sunk so low that even these—" She gave Laney an unreadable glance. "—children could stop you?"

81

As if choreographed, several of Arthur's lieutenants, armed with AK-47s, sprang from various hiding places in the room. Another half-dozen men stepped from the shadows, protecting Larisa, aiming their guns in response.

Checkmate.

The band trembled, except for Greg and Mitch. They'd both cheated death before. It had been a good run while it lasted.

"You say I'm stupid, right? I don't go anywhere without preparation, honey!" Arthur brayed. "Sorry our partnership has to end this way, but you tell your boys to back the fuck up. You know damn well that I should have been promoted out of this shithole!"

Arthur and his crew closed ranks, eyes locked on Larisa's crew. Arthur backed toward the fire exit. Two armed men held it open for him, ready to gun down anyone who'd try to stop them. Arthur turned to exit into the back alley and froze. His hands rose as if of their own accord, fingers splayed.

"Trouble" Macintyre stood outside the fire door with a leather-clad crowd of his biker brothers. Johnny held a custom-made M203 grenade launcher with fold-out stock. Easy to conceal, nasty to deploy. A tad overstated, but Johnny wasn't a firm believer in subtlety. Arthur's heavies backed into The Hotseat with their boss squirming between them.

From the front doorway behind where Larisa's men stood, there came a wet clubbing sound. One of her men dropped like a stone. It was Larisa's turn to freeze up.

The band turned to see their rescuers, friends and neighbors of Martin's, armed with a variety of weapons. Blood trickled down a Louisville slugger from the fist of Andre Brooks, Martin's cousin.

"'Scuse me, wuz it you ordered the Soul food?"

They forced Larisa's toughs deeper into the club, next to Arthur's, herding them against the bar like penned sheep. Though sheep armed with automatic weapons.

Bikers to the left, brothers to the right. Here they were, stuck together in the middle.

"Tha's it! Git together for a group photo an' smile, motherfuckers! C'mon, cuz. Y'all move, move!"

Laney, no longer giving a damn, pointed two fingers at her eyes, then the same fingers at Arthur, the "I see you!" stare before she raced out of the closing ring of armed and angry men, leading the rest of the band through a door at the back. They rushed single file between towering stacks of beer and pop cases.

On his way through, Mitch snatched a six-pack of pop from an open case.

Once outside, everybody scattered. Mitch popped the tops off a pair of twenty ounce bottles. He shook them, thumbs pressed over the openings. The two Russians left behind to watch the back door, cautiously peered out the open windows of the limo, only to be met with concussive blasts of pent-up fizz. Mitch's Hail Mary pass was just enough to cause confusion and gain some distance.

Gunfire erupted from the interior of the limo. Blind

snapshots flying wild; striking the floor and walls of the alley. Buzzing away in all directions like pissed-off supersonic bees. The band hauled ass to their van, covered by Martin's kinfolk. The brothers boiled out of the store room door, keeping their guns trained on the pair of soda-soaked Russians. The element of surprise had run its course.

The fact remained that the combined collection of Russians had them outgunned. It was time to leave, and quick. Once they shut the heavy door, agitated *pokk-pokk*-ing sounds from within dimpled the steel clad surface. The door exploded open, propelled by the weight of outraged Russians. The Cossacks had been slowed down, but once outside, they broke into a full charge, which made their aim sloppy.

The brothers went full-sprint, occasionally returning fire. The Russians were closing the gap on the brothers until a blinding explosion separated the two camps. Gravel and dust spewed thirty feet in the air. From the other side of the alley, Johnny's spent grenade launcher left a ribbon of smoke trailing skyward. His biker crew let out howls of laughter like drunken desperados.

Ian swung open the van's back door, causing a landslide of guitars to tumble out of the van. He leapt head first, as if he were flying. The band did a head count. Everyone was aboard but Laney. She climbed in last, snatching her guitar from the pile in the alley.

Out of nowhere, Todd frantically charged to the van, blocking the back door from closing.

"Laney, hold up! I got enough good shit to get us cross-country if we need to."

"Oh, now you show up," Greg said.

"Come with me, babe, the fucking ax is about to fall!"

The ax that fell was Laney's guitar connecting with Todd's face.

"Greg may be an asshole, but he's our asshole!"

Todd landed hard on his ass, stunned.

All doors of the van slammed shut. Ian started up the van and fishtailed out of the back lot leaving Todd, the wrong brand of asshole, coughing in a cloud of blue exhaust.

82

The Demands, Johnny's crew and Martin's crew were long gone before a convoy of police cars, drawn by Johnny's explosion, skidded, sirens blaring and lights spinning, into the parking lot. Arthur's buddies couldn't cover for him now, not in front of superiors.

83

Miles away, Ian continued driving with ferocity, scanning the roads ahead like a sharpshooter to avoid being stopped. His foot never left the gas pedal and his hands kept their death grip on the wheel. Stop lights meant nothing now. He darted around oncoming traffic, trailed by car horns. Frank Bullitt had the open roads of San Fran, not the pockmarked cork-screws of Pittsburgh. Ian continued to fly past one township after another while his passengers braced themselves against anything steady—the driver's seat, the walls, each other. Ian threaded the needle between a parked car and a fire hydrant, to make as sharp a turn as he could. He didn't know if the mob were following and he wasn't about to look behind to find out.

"Jeee-zus H. motherfucking Christ! You're gonna kill us!" Mitch screamed.

"Shuddup! And tell me if you see someone coming!"

The fuel gauge was well into the red.

Ian knew all the roads not usually travelled. Secluded, wooded nooks where they might lie low for the night. Once off the main roads, he swerved up steep and dangerous slopes. The zig-zagging tossed the band about like a rattled ant farm. When Ian finally stopped, they were a tangled dog-pile strewn amongst the remaining instruments.

84

They had landed at the top of the aptly named Fineview. It was a goat path alley tottering along the hillside, a remote spot overlooking Pittsburgh. Just to be on the safe side, Ian stuck the van amongst the shrubbery. 600 feet above sea level was enough, he thought.

One by one, the band wriggled out, woozy from their spin-cycle escape. The chill of the night air helped them regain some clarity and footing. Laney wobbled like a puppet until she dropped on the damp grass, facing the city lights below.

Woozy or not, she could see how splendid her adopted hometown looked from her perch. It helped her mind shed off the vertigo.

"Wow, you can see for miles up here. So pretty at night," Laney said.

The sound of Mitch throwing up, his adrenaline spent, broke the solemnity of the mood. Paul helped Mitch to his feet.

Sticks snapped and weeds thrashed a few yards away from them.

"Dude, can't keep up?" said someone in the shadows.

"Cut this dude off, man," said another.

The band didn't recognize the voices and expected the worst. Greg and Martin were barely on their feet but ready for a fight.

Three heads poked out in the moonlight. They were college boys in their alma mater jackets. All three had tall beer cans clasped in their hands. This was most likely their hideaway to drink.

"I'm good," Mitch said, wiping away small flecks of vomit with his sleeve.

"Got any more o' those?" said Paul.

"Sure. We brought plenty." One of them went back to get more beer while introductions were made. A large cooler was placed by the van.

Snap-fsssk!

"Up your ass, Ian."

"No, up yours, Mitch, I insist."

T-tunk!

Beer was flowing and the mood of the band slowly eased from edginess to hilarity. Hours later, Laney was wearing one of the student's jackets to shake off the cold. Martin, Greg and Jason fell asleep in the van.

85

"Ian was all like, whoosh, whoosh, outttamyway!" Laney gleefully said before rolling over, holding her stomach, laughing. She let out a giant snort, which led to more laughter. After all that had happened, the thought of winning over the crowd at The Hotseat seemed so . . . dumb. She was having giggle fits she thought would never stop. What a trip.

One student crouched down to where Mitch lay and offered him another beer.

"Dude, y'gotta promise us, since we are, like, bonded by beer, that we keep this spot our little secret, 'kay."

"My new friend, I can—*bruuuupt*—assure you that we are the very best at keeping secrets."

Acknowledgements

Acknowledgements and special thanks: Chuck Dixon, Karen Geraci, Sean Hoffman, Jeremy Puckett, Deerwood McCord, Rick Sofilkanich, Craig Norkus, Gary J. Sella, Paula J. Ciccimarra Sella, James Lunt, WDVE, Dave Grohl, Christopher Kozak, Frank Alansky, Karen Klickovich, Donald Klickovich, Carolyn Franklin, Henry Koerner, Karen Danzelli, Alisande Morales, Dave Johnson, David Wright, Ben Abernathy, Keith Barnett, Rob Hunter, Howard Porter, Tom Nguyen, Samulel L. McBrayer, John Dell, Derec Donovan, Justin Walner, Dusty Abell, Sergio Cariello, Jeannie Schwartz, Anne L. McCullough, Michael Wright, English Nick, Ray Davies, Dave Davies, Mike Carlin, Bob Layton, Jordan B. Gorfinkel, Fran Ferragonio, Robert McMullen, Taluna McMullen, Sheri Kelly, Gary Kelly, Phil Evans, Jason Armstrong, Chris Drysdale, Sky Drysdale, Robert Geraci, Patricia Geraci, Lawrence Geraci, and Jaye Manus for enduring my endless questions.

About the Author

Drew Geraci has been in the advertising and entertainment industry for thirty years, with international clients that include Disney Publishing Worldwide, Marvel Studios, Marvel Entertainment, DC Entertainment and more. Credits include articles for *Sketch Magazine* and promotional artwork for *Star Wars, Mass Effect, Batman, The Avengers* and *Guardians of The Galaxy*. He has taught creative workshops, did a guest stint as a disc jockey . . . and danced onstage with Iggy Pop.

Contact Drew Geraci
www.drewgeraciauthor.com
www.drewgeraci.com
Facebook: drew.geraci1
Facebook: The-Demands

45046607R00126

Made in the USA
Lexington, KY
19 September 2015